NAKED EYE

Check out this thrilling new series:

FEARLESS® FBI

FEARLESS FBI

NAKED EYE

Francine Pascal

SIMON PULSE
New York London Toronto Sydney

First Simon Pulse edition June 2006

SIMON PULSE
An imprint of Simon & Schuster Children's Publishing Division
1230 Avenue of the Americas, New York, NY 10020

Produced by Alloy Entertainment
151 West 26th Street
New York, NY 10001

Printed in the United States of America
10 9 8 7 6 5 4 3 2 1

Library of Congress Control Number: 2005933888
ISBN-13: 978-0-689-87824-4
ISBN-10: 0-689-87824-9

NAKED EYE

Gaia

I had been keeping an audio log of the past forty-eight hours. A way to organize my thoughts and keep myself company—as well as keep myself focused and awake. Right now it's sitting in the glove box of Catherine's Altima. If I don't survive the next few hours (and that's looking more and more likely), I'm sure the FBI will eventually find it and dissect it. I hope it will explain everything for them. Why I went AWOL. Why I evaded arrest. Why I didn't contact them with my leads.

I only wish I could make one more entry. If I had that recorder with me in this dusty, dim cellar and the Vin Diesel look-alike with the Ruger pointed at me could somehow find it in his heart to untape my mouth, this is what I would say:

I'm sorry.

I'm not sorry I followed up on Catherine's disappearance because I was right, after all, that something sinister was up. I just never imagined that Catherine was a part of it. What I am sorry for is not trusting Malloy, Bishop, and the whole FBI system. I let my frustration over the way Cathy's case was handled resurrect the cynical, loner Gaia, teenager Gaia, the Gaia who found it difficult to trust the CIA and even her own father.

I'd probably also say I'm sorry that I never got the chance to talk to my father and ask him the questions I've been lugging around inside me for years. Like . . . why couldn't he just be a dad after Mom died? And whether or not he sees any of Mom in me.

I'd explain how sorry I am that I can't hang out with my brother, D., one last time on his farm, watching him milk cows and cuddle the baby chicks. I'd tell him to stay sweet and innocent and not to be sad for me. I chose this life. So I guess I chose this death, too.

Then, last but not least, I'd say how more than anything I'm sorry I dragged Will into this. I'd explain how he risked everything to come here to help me and how he tried to convince me to contact the authorities, but I wouldn't listen.

I keep trying to tell him I'm sorry with my eyes, but he barely looks at me. He keeps focusing on the men watching over us. No, not the men. The guns. He's scared. Only he doesn't want me to see it.

And that's something else I'm sorry about. I'm sorry I was born fearless. It's always been my curse. Because I'm this freak of nature, it seems people I care about are always at risk. But maybe that'll be something good that comes out of my demise. Maybe my friends and family can finally be safe.

I don't fear the end—I don't fear anything. I only wish it didn't have to be like this.

worst nightmare, part two

Stupid, nameless, fatigue-wearing, gun-toting thugs! They were all alike.

Gaia fought the urge to struggle as two muscle-bound creeps tied her up. They'd already finished with her ankles and were now working on her arms, securing them behind her back with several tight loops around her waist. It was more effective than the standard, run-of-the-mill wrist bindings but also uncomfortable as hell. If it hadn't been for the strip of duct tape over her lips and the fact that she was cooperating nicely for Will's safety's sake, she would have let loose a barrage of colorful curse words.

As soon as the two brutes finished with her, they turned to help their comrades truss up Will, who *was* resisting. One held the gun up against Will's skull as another bound his ankles and two others secured his arms. It hurt to see the fear in Will's eyes. Gaia felt a pain in the center of her chest, as if her heart was a rotating saw slowly shredding her with every beat. This was all her fault.

It was like Jake all over again. Her worst nightmare, part two.

Jake . . . It was hard to picture her former boyfriend the way he'd usually been: smiling and cocksure. Instead she could only picture him the way he'd looked in his last few minutes of life. Gasping and blood soaked, staring at her urgently, his broad chest torn to shreds.

Not again, she thought. It wasn't so much a lamentation as it was an order—to herself. *It will* not *happen again!* She had to get Will out of here or die trying.

As soon as they were done tying Will up, the biggest hoodlum shoved him to the concrete floor. Gaia strained futilely against the ropes around her waist. *Leave him alone!* she wanted to yell. But all she could manage was a long, laser-eyed death stare.

Stupid thugs! Where did they learn how to bind people's hands so well anyway? Maybe this was what happened to Boy Scouts gone bad. They all grew up to become cronies for megalomaniac terrorists. That way they could get some use out of their extensive knot-tying skills. Plus, like these guys, they still got to wear uniforms. Only instead of khakis with jaunty neckerchiefs, the men who worked for Winston Marsh all had on black T-shirts and camouflage pants. Standard-issue revolutionary gear.

Once Gaia and Will were bound and taped, two of the men left through the steel doors to the main bunker, leaving behind the baldest, brawniest brute as guard and sentry.

Gaia sat back against the rough-hewn wall and took note of their surroundings. They were in a narrow anteroom, just off the main chamber of Socorro's headquarters—a bunker three stories below street level in Philadelphia. Like the other room, this one had rough concrete walls bolstered by metal girders. At one end was the thick steel door they'd just been led through. And at the other end, the end closest to Gaia, was a corroded metal ladder extending upward. She couldn't see where it led, but if she just leaned a little to the right, she might be able to catch a glimpse of the top.

Making sure the bulldog-faced guard wasn't watching too

intently, Gaia slanted her body sideways until she could see the ladder as it disappeared into a tunnel in the ceiling. But she couldn't see the top. The rungs stretched up into darkness.

Suddenly something hard struck her in the chest. *"Enderécese! Get back up!"* snarled the guard, kicking her again with the toe of his boot.

Will let out a loud grunt behind his duct tape and flailed against his bindings, his eyes projecting pure rage at the guard. The guard spun toward him, ready to strike Will's skull with the base of his rifle, but Gaia twisted her torso around and quickly brought up her legs, crashing her shins into the guard's heels. The man lost his footing and fell backward with a surprised cry, his gun clattering across the floor.

"What's going on in here?" A man pushed open the steel door and glared around the room, his rifle at the ready.

It was James Rossiter, Marsh's favorite go-to guy—and Gaia's least favorite of the thugs. She noticed he'd tried desperately to squeeze his paunch into the same military fatigues the others wore, but it looked more like a mottled potato sack on his stocky frame. Yet even though Rossiter wasn't as lean or athletic as the others, he was still a force to be reckoned with. Her throat probably still had marks from their brutal tangle two days earlier.

Rossiter looked down at the sprawled, dazed form of the guard, then over at Will, who was scrabbling on the floor, trying to get to his feet.

"You little . . ." Rossiter stalked over and kicked Will hard in the ribs.

Gaia screamed in anger from beneath the tape and Rossiter spun around toward her.

"Well, well . . . lookee here," he said with a sneer. "I'm going to enjoy this." He shouldered his rifle by the strap, reached down with one hand, and pulled Gaia off the floor by her hair. A searing pain swept down from her scalp as her torso rose up off the ground. She watched Rossiter ball up his other hand into a meaty fist and saw Will thrash in helpless anger out of the corner of her eye. *Fine,* she thought as she lifted her chin and waited for the eventual collision.

"Jimmy?" came an unctuous male voice, interrupting Rossiter's punch. Winston Marsh stood in the doorway, surveying the scene. "How are our guests?" he asked matter-of-factly, as if he were the host of a twisted cocktail party.

Rossiter released Gaia and let her collapse in a heap to the concrete. "I caught them causing trouble," he snarled. "They took down Diego." He gestured toward the guard who was stumbling awkwardly to his feet.

"Ah, I see." Marsh nodded briskly. "It's okay, Jimmy. I'll handle it. Get your team ready. You leave for the courthouse in a few minutes."

Rossiter grunted his assent and, after a final glower at Gaia, walked out of the room.

As soon as he was gone, Marsh strode over to Gaia and bent over her, resting his hands on his knees. She glared back at him, her pent-up fury scorching her eyes.

"This rage you're feeling toward us, Gaia, it's a natural response," he said smoothly. "Unwise, but natural. That is another reason why Ramon is so special. He never gives in to the anger."

Gaia's frustration continued to build. Ah, the famous, Ramon Nino—head of Socorro's network of terrorists and current federal prisoner who was slated to be brought to court that day. She'd wondered when they would get around to discussing him.

"Ramon reaches out to his captors as well as his fellow prisoners, spreading his message," Marsh continued. "Diego here was in prison with him in Bogotá. And Luis and Ignacio were former guards. All of us were enlightened by his message of truth."

Gaia stared into Marsh's steely blue eyes. He was so calm, so cool. Within the first hour of her meeting Marsh, he'd begun lecturing her in that voice of his—with its hypnotic, resounding tone, like that of a Shakespearean actor or an insurance commercial narrator. The kind of voice that made him seem wiser than everyone, even when all he was doing was ordering a cup of coffee.

It was hard for Gaia to believe she'd initially welcomed his advice. But after searching for Catherine for several hours, followed by an embarrassing run-in with James Rossiter, she had been too full of self-doubt to question him. Now, though, his smooth tones just pissed her off.

"It gives me no pleasure to see you like this, Gaia," Marsh continued in a lower octave, his eyes round with fatherly pity. "I would rather you be at my side, working with Catherine as a friend and comrade. A sister, even."

Gaia felt a tiny tug behind her rib cage. The word *sister* uncorked some bottled-up emotions. She knew he was trying to convince her to endorse his warped schemes, but the thought of being reunited with Catherine, of partnering with her again, still appealed to Gaia on a subconscious level.

Marsh somehow read this in her eyes. "I know you missed her. And she's missed you. She thinks so highly of you, Gaia. Your intellect, strength, loyalty. But more than that, she really feels a

9

bond with you. Why else would we go to all this trouble to bring you here?"

To trap me, Gaia answered silently. *Just like all the other nutcases in my past. You wanted a piece of the fearless girl.*

"It wasn't a trap, Gaia," Marsh went on, once again reading her thoughts. "It was a test. To see if you really were as ingenious and capable as Catherine had said you were. And you passed. Quite tremendously, I might add. We were all very impressed."

Oh, yes, she was quite the bounty hunter. She'd trekked across three states, tangled with FBI agents on her tail, abandoned her hunt for the Lollipop Killer, and broken a pack of laws and regulations in an effort to find her friend. And she had found her. Right here, three stories beneath the streets of Philadelphia. With her psycho daddy and his pet gunmen. Ready to carry out an insurgent kidnapping plot they'd been planning for months. And the worst of it was, they'd been expecting her.

So forgive me if I don't feel I deserve a pat on the back.

"Catherine!" Marsh shouted through the open door. "Come here, please."

A second later Catherine trotted into the room and stood next to her father. "Yes?" she said, adjusting her glasses. Her big, round eyes gazed about the room, taking in the scene: the guard, still shaking his head and rubbing his neck; Will coughing and sputtering behind his tape; and Gaia, sprawled sideways on the concrete like a bag of dirty laundry. Gaia couldn't be sure, but she thought she saw the tiniest, most fleeting look of regret on Catherine's elfin features.

"Can't we at least take the tape off her mouth?" Catherine frowned.

"Now, Catherine. I'm surprised at you. You're a very smart girl, but you're not thinking about this the right way," Marsh said in an admonishing yet fatherly tone, as if he were discussing a disappointing report card or a chore left undone. "I don't like treating Gaia this way any more than you. But we should leave her gagged, at least for now. That way she will have no choice but to listen to us. To the truth."

"I guess you're right," Catherine replied. She hung her head slightly, gazing down at her hands.

Even after everything she'd gone through, Gaia still felt a twinge of empathy. Catherine was obviously a victim of her own upbringing. Instead of recruiting the perfect soldier, her father had made one, straight from his own loins. She could only imagine what Catherine's childhood must have been like. The lessons and drills. The constant brainwashing.

"What about him?" Catherine lifted her chin toward Will.

"Don't bother with him. He will be killed in a matter of minutes."

Gaia started to struggle, and Catherine placed a hand on her shoulder. "But we need him," she said to her father. "If only to make Gaia cooperate."

Marsh looked from Gaia to Will and back again. "You're right. That's my girl." He reached out and patted Catherine lightly on the back. "Talk to her, Cathy. Show her the way," he instructed. "I've got to go over details one last time with Jimmy."

"Yes, sir," Catherine said.

Marsh gave his daughter a peck on the cheek and headed out of the room.

"I'm so pleased you're here with us, Gaia," Catherine began as soon as he left. "We're giving you an incredible opportunity. I know you joined the FBI to help people, but with us you can help millions. And you can use *all* of your unique talents. You won't be held back by needless rules."

Gaia stared at her in disbelief. Did Catherine really think she was going to buy into this nonsense?

"I'm going to describe some of the horrible atrocities that have happened to our people," Catherine said, sitting cross-legged on the floor next to Gaia as if they were chatting around a campfire. "I don't have time to go over everything, but when you hear what I have to say, I'm sure it will change your mind about us. You're a good person, Gaia. I know you'll agree that something has to be done."

Wow. She really *did* think it was that simple. And why not? Catherine had seen Gaia struggle against FBI rules all through training. Marsh had personally witnessed her taking down an FBI agent sent to capture her. And they already seemed to know about her loner vigilante days. So of course they figured she was a prime candidate to be brainwashed against the government.

Gaia kept staring at Catherine as she talked. There was something familiar about her wild-eyed expression, something that hit very close to home. Suddenly she realized who it reminded her of: Loki. Her brilliant, criminally insane uncle. He was always able to rationalize doing horrible acts in the name of a "greater good." Using only words, he could twist the most abhorrent crime into something brave and valiant. In his mind he was prophetic, not psychotic—a harbinger of the future, not of doom and despair. Catherine, it seemed, wore a similar pair of rose-colored terrorist glasses.

Which gave Gaia an idea . . .

Maybe this could end up working in our favor. If there was one good thing about Gaia's screwed-up childhood, it was that she'd gotten very good at dealing with villainous crackpots. All she had to do was make Catherine think she was winning her over—not too easily, but enough to make her lower her defenses.

It would require an Academy Award–winning performance, but Gaia could do it. After all, it might at least buy her enough time to figure out an escape plan.

THE HOLE AT THE END OF THE BARREL

Will stared at Gaia with equal parts awe and annoyance. It was unnerving to see her registering zero fear, despite the fact that they were in a place no one knew about, surrounded by armed brutes. And not only did she seem all la-di-da about the whole trapped-in-terrorist-headquarters aspect of their situation, she was actually listening to Catherine yammer on and on as if they were sharing secrets at a slumber party.

Don't mind me, y'all, he thought as he struggled to a sitting position. *You gals keep visiting. I'll just kick back and take a nap.*

If he could have, he would have joked aloud. It was his thing. The way he always steadied his nerves. Only this time it wasn't working—aloud or silently.

Will groaned and banged his head gently against the rough steel-and-concrete wall. He was hungry, tired, frustrated as hell, and barely keeping his panic in check. And Gaia was suddenly more interested in her terrorist former roommate than in helping them escape. As he shifted into a more comfortable position, he kept a close eye on the gun in the guard's right hand. It was aimed right at him, the hole at the end of the barrel making a perfect dot in the distance.

A Ruger, he surmised. *A 556, to be exact.*

He'd gone hunting a few times as a boy. Although he'd never shot any game, he had gotten pretty good at knocking Coke cans off the fence. Now, after his training at the bureau, he had expert aim and could take apart and reassemble his firearm like a pro. All in all, he had a pretty solid relationship with guns. There was only one problem: he'd never actually had a loaded one pointed *at* him . . .

Until now.

Will fixed his gaze on the sleek chrome barrel. He couldn't help imagining the bullet discharging toward him, shattering his skull and spewing his brain matter all over the floor of the bunker. And there was nothing he could do. He had about as much power as one of those empty soda cans on the backyard fence.

He wrenched his eyes off the Ruger and stared again at Gaia, who was still listening to Catherine, nodding like a kid at storytime.

She isn't afraid, he kept thinking as he watched her. *How can she not be afraid?*

He remembered how his mom pretended to be strong and unafraid. She had always been so determined to do everything herself—almost as if she wanted to prove to the world that she didn't need a man. Will used to think Gaia was like that. But for her it wasn't an act. Right this moment they were in the clutches of an armed militia and no one knew where the hell they were. Yet she wasn't the least bit shaky. Her eyes were focused, her breathing regular. She had told him before that she was fearless, but now he could *see* it.

It was amazing but also intimidating as hell.

Just stay focused, he told himself, trying to remember his training. *Stay aware of your surroundings.* He forced himself to look away from the gun and from Gaia. Instead he gazed out the open doorway into the main bunker. The pudgy guy, Jimmy, was leaving with three other henchmen, no doubt heading up the tunnels toward the courthouse to retrieve Nino. That left only Marsh, Catherine, and two other lackeys, including their guard.

At least the numbers were thinning. Things were slightly less hopeless.

If only he could find a weapon or send a distress call or hypnotize one of the gunmen into helping them. Anything that could give them a real chance. If he and Gaia were going to make a break, they had to do it before Jimmy's bunch returned.

Of course, there was still the little matter of their bindings. Not to mention all the loaded guns and stockpile of plastic explosives.

It seemed like his FBI training should have prepared him for this. But he must have missed the lecture on how to keep from freaking when you're hog-tied, outnumbered, outgunned, and dizzy from lack of sleep.

Will slouched back and leaned his head against the metal joist. *Ow!* he cried silently as something sharp poked his forearm. Glancing down, he saw a rough, serrated corner where the steel beam disappeared into the concrete floor.

Great. Now not only was he tired, hungry, and freaked, he was practically impaling himself against a wall of jagged spikes. If he wasn't careful, he could end up slicing open his skin.

A sudden realization swept through him, revving the tempo of his heartbeat. Leaning against the wall, he cautiously rubbed his arm against the rough spot again. Yes, it was sharp. Very sharp.

Sharp enough to slice through rope.

THEY DON'T TAKE HOSTAGES

Kim sat across from Special Agent Malloy, trying to stop his leg from bouncing nervously. It worked—for a few seconds. Then his heel would start tapping against the carpeting again.

It didn't help that he'd been escorted from the brig to the office by a pair of burly jarheads armed with automatic weapons, one of whom now stood to his left and the other in the hall by the door. Nor did it help that his commanding officer was shooting him a look of such intense fury, Kim wouldn't have been surprised to see steam billow from his nostrils. Malloy was an intimidating man to begin with. When angered, he was just scary as hell.

"Agent Lau, is it possible that someone with your intelligence would not grasp the magnitude of the situation you are in?" Malloy paused to take a breath, using it to amp up his volume even more. "Ignoring regulations, circumventing security, accessing top secret clearance files, and helping a fellow trainee go AWOL! Am I forgetting anything?"

Nope. That just about covers it. Understanding that the question was rhetorical, Kim kept his mouth shut.

Malloy turned and shared a glance with Special Agent Bishop. She raised her eyebrows and shook her head. Kim knew the base's second in command was just as angry and just as capable of making someone squirm as her louder, coarser superior.

"While you have been sitting in the holding cell, my men have been reviewing security tapes and data records," Malloy restarted. "We know Agent Taylor called up files on Ramon Nino and his group Socorro."

Kim stared back at him, trying to look like he was hearing all this for the first time. Will had told him about Socorro taking Catherine and how Gaia had tracked them down. He'd also discovered evidence of a bomb—something even Gaia had been unaware of. Will had left to warn her and Kim had covered for him, knowing full well it would lead to this very meeting with a fire-breathing Malloy.

Because when Catherine had gone missing, Kim, like Gaia, had also been frustrated at the bureau's official findings. Their explanation that she'd been abducted and killed just didn't make sense. Who kidnapped someone from a heavily armed base? If it was information they wanted, why not nab Malloy or Bishop, someone actually privy to highly classified files? So, when an agent as smart and dedicated as Gaia went AWOL as part of an apparent quest to find Catherine, Kim realized something even more insidious might be at work. Gaia either thought that the bureau was too inept to find Catherine or, even worse, that they didn't *want* to find her. And Kim wasn't going to be the only one in their group who didn't lift a finger to help.

Kim glanced at the clock on the wall. He wondered if Will had made it to Gaia yet with the information. Somehow he was sure he had. He just prayed they found and dismantled the bomb in time.

"Agent Lau?" Bishop stepped forward and placed her palms on the desk, leaning toward Kim. "What you might not realize is that right this minute, Ramon Nino is being transferred to a Philadelphia courthouse for his parole hearing. We've had intel for some time that Socorro might be planning something to coincide with this court date. If you know anything, it is imperative that you tell us. An organization as deadly as Socorro is far too dangerous for two agents in training to take on alone. These people have left entire city blocks in rubble. They don't claim responsibility, they don't grandstand, and they don't take hostages."

Kim's eyes widened. "They don't?" he blurted, unable to stop himself from interrupting.

Malloy glared at him, his face turning the color of raw hamburger meat. "No, Lau! That is *not* their MO! These people recruit folks from the cradle and train them to destroy and kill in the name of their organization. They move in, do as much damage as they can, and move out. They don't take prisoners!"

Kim's gut clenched and a stinging, watery film covered his eyes. If Catherine wasn't Socorro's hostage, she must already be dead. And that meant Gaia and Will were walking into a trap.

This revelation changed everything.

Malloy rose to his feet, his figure cutting an enormous shadow out of the sunlight that spilled into the room from the window behind him. "Forget your own future for a moment, Agent Lau. If you think you are somehow helping your friends, you are sorely mistaken. And unless you want their blood on your head, I suggest you start telling me everything that you know."

Kim's mind raced and his eyes darted around the room, as if looking for a sign. *What the hell should I do? If I spill my guts, the FBI might haul them in and toss them in the brig beside me before they'd have a chance to rescue Catherine. But if Malloy's right and I do nothing —*

"I don't have time for this nonsense!" Malloy boomed. "Guard, take this man to—"

"Wait!" Kim rose to his feet. "I'll help you. I'll tell you what I know. But you have to promise me you won't punish them!"

Malloy and Bishop exchanged a brief, indecipherable look. Then Bishop approached Kim and placed her hand on his arm. "Agent Lau, this loyalty you feel for your fellow trainees . . . what makes you think we don't feel it toward all of you?"

DETONATE

"And they actually decided it would be cheaper and better for the company to pay a measly death benefit to the victims' families than to actually overhaul their factories and make them safe!" Catherine concluded, her voice shaky with indignation.

Gaia stiffened as if incensed. She stared off into the distance, shaking her head. It hadn't been difficult at all to appear shocked and saddened at the stories Catherine told. If she hadn't been bound and gagged and forced to listen at gunpoint, she might have been horrified enough to take some action. But right then the only thing she was purely focused on was escape.

That and the fact that she couldn't find a comfortable position.

There was an intense pain in her shoulders from her arms being tied behind her back. The ropes around her midsection were so tight, it hurt to take deep breaths. She hoped Will was faring better.

19

Pretending to stretch, she craned her neck and stole a quick glance toward Will. His shoulders were shaking slightly. Then she zeroed in on the minor back-and-forth motion of his hands behind his back. He must have found a sharp spot! He was cutting the bindings!

Their eyes meet briefly and Will gave her a quick, almost imperceptible wink of his left eye, acknowledging his plan. *I could kiss you right now, Will Taylor. If we weren't surrounded by armed radicals.*

Getting out of here would be much easier if Will were untied. Now all she had to do was make sure Catherine and the pinhead guard didn't realize what he was up to.

She shifted sideways, blocking Will so that all they could see were his legs. Then she arched her back and moaned behind her tape. She had to keep the focus on her as much as possible.

"Gaia?" Catherine stopped talking and studied her. Her expression softened and the manic glint in her eye switched to low beam. "I'm sorry. I know it hurts." She glanced over her shoulder into the adjoining room. "Dad?" she called.

"Yes?"

"Can I let loose a couple of her bindings?

Marsh strode toward them, studying Gaia intently. "Did you talk to her, Cathy?"

"Yes."

"And?"

Catherine looked into Gaia's eyes and smiled. "She sees, Dad. I can tell she sees. Just like I told you, she could be a reformer in no time."

Marsh nodded slowly. "Cut loose her feet and untape her

mouth. But Gaia"—he leaned toward her with his hands on his knees—"just so you know, if Diego sees you try anything against me or Cathy, he will instantly kill your friend." He gave her a warm, almost sympathetic smile and then returned to the main bunker, rejoining the other henchmen.

"I knew you'd understand," Catherine said excitedly, giving Gaia's arm a little squeeze. "I knew it the moment I met you." She turned toward the guard. "Diego, *deme el puñal.*"

The man unclipped a sheath on his belt and pulled out a knife, which he slid, handle forward, across the floor to her.

"Gracias." She leaned over and began slicing through the bindings around Gaia's ankles. "This is going to be perfect. We'll be partners again."

Gaia felt a squeezing sensation behind her ribs. In a strange way, she felt like the villain now. She hated to deceive Catherine. But she had to do whatever was necessary to ensure Will wasn't killed.

As soon as she had cut Gaia's ankle bindings, Catherine returned the knife to the guard and helped Gaia to her feet. "Brace yourself," she said, grabbing a corner of the tape. "Ready?"

Gaia nodded. In one quick motion Catherine yanked the tape off her mouth, and Gaia felt simultaneous pain and relief.

"Come on," Catherine said, leading her into the bunker.

Gaia leaned on her, pretending to be slightly wobbly on her feet. With her legs freed, she could now make her move at any time. But first she had to make sure Will was out of immediate danger.

"Ah, Miss Moore," Marsh greeted as they hobbled into the room. "Won't you have a seat?" He gestured to a wooden crate across from him. Gaia settled onto it, trying to look weary and slightly humbled.

21

"I'm glad that you are beginning to see the light," he went on. "Very soon you will meet Ramon and everything will become clear."

A loud crackling noise suddenly emanated from Marsh's walkie-talkie, cutting him off. Marsh grabbed up the unit and fiddled with the volume knob. Soon Rossiter's gruff tones sputtered from the small speaker.

"Marsh! You there?"

"Jimmy," Marsh responded. "Have you reached the courthouse?"

"Yeah, but we've got trouble! Two trucks have pulled up outside and the FBI is swarming the building!"

Marsh whirled around and glowered at Will. Gaia turned, too, afraid Marsh might see Will cutting the ropes. But Will was still slumped in the corner, looking sullen.

"Has Ramon arrived?" Marsh shouted into the walkie-talkie.

"His car pulled up right before the trucks," came Rossiter's staticky reply.

Marsh rubbed his chin for a moment before pressing the call button once again. "They may still go ahead with the hearing, using the agents for extra security," he said to Rossiter. "Wait thirty minutes. If he comes into the building, grab him. If not, the three of you are to return to base. Do not let anyone discover the tunnel access point!"

"Roger that." The walkie-talkie hissed and snapped a few more times before going silent.

Marsh let out a string of curse words and turned to one of the guards. "Luis! Get to the street and see about the vehicles." The man nodded and scurried out of the tunnel. Marsh then rounded on Catherine. "Arm the explosives!" he snapped.

Catherine's mouth fell open. "But they have a thirty-minute countdown! What if Ramon is in the tunnels when they detonate?"

"Then we will honor him by making him a martyr!" Marsh's blue eyes grew wide, and his voice was charged with an almost religious fervor.

Catherine stood staring at him for a moment, wringing her hands with worry.

"Do as I said!" he cried.

"Yes, sir." She scurried off toward another crate and opened it up, revealing a pile of radio equipment.

Two against three, Gaia thought as she watched Catherine carefully set down her gun. *The odds just keep getting better.*

"Well, Miss Moore." Marsh stood in front of her, pistol in hand. His eyes looked much less guppyish, but his words still had a sizzling, ferocious quality to them. "We must leave our headquarters a little sooner than expected. Either join us or stay behind and perish when the explosives take down this bunker. We will not force you to leave."

Gaia paused. If only she knew how Will was doing with his ropes. "What about my friend?" she asked, buying time.

He shook his head as if in regret. "I'm afraid you can't save him. But why should you die needlessly?"

Again she paused, weighing her options. There was no room for error.

She felt she stood a solid chance against Marsh and Catherine, even with both hands literally tied behind her back. After all, Marsh wasn't exactly a role model for physical fitness. But what about Will? The guard still had him in his sights.

Just then Will coughed. He could have just been clearing his lungs of the dust and grime swirling through the air. Or could it be more than that?

Could he be trying to send her a signal?

ONE STRAY BULLET

Will sat stiffly, holding his arms behind him as if they were still bound together. He hoped Gaia had picked up his message, but he couldn't tell for sure. She was just so unflinching.

His shoulders ached from straining against the bindings, but luckily he was free. Or half free, anyway. He had only managed to slice through one of the loops and wrangle his left hand loose. But that was enough. It would have to be.

"Well, Miss Moore?" Marsh was still standing in front of Gaia, yammering on in that gospel preacher voice of his. "What will it be?"

Gaia tilted her head as if pondering the matter deeply.

"Maybe I should illustrate your options more clearly," Marsh cut in, sounding slightly impatient. He turned and called to the guard. "Diego! Bring the prisoner!"

The burly guy grinned a predatory grin as he loped toward Will. *Stay cool,* Will told himself as his heart thrashed madly inside him. *Wait for just the right moment.* With one hand and both feet still tied, he couldn't win a struggle. He had to take the guard out with one single, perfect blow.

Diego crept closer and closer until he was finally standing directly in front of him. *Almost . . . Wait for it. . . .*

"Get up," Diego commanded.

Will glared at him. He pretended to try to rise and then slumped back as if frustrated.

Diego laughed. *"Pobrecito,"* he mocked. "Poor baby." He shouldered his semiautomatic and leaned over Will, getting ready to hoist him to his feet.

Now!

As soon as Diego bent forward, Will shot his left hand up at full force, crashing the bony edge into the man's larynx. Diego stared wide-eyed at him for a second and then collapsed to the floor, gasping and clutching at his throat. Will lunged forward and grabbed his weapon, yanking it off his struggling body. Then he tore the tape from his mouth.

"Gaia!" Will cried as he pulled the gun strap over his head and fingered the firing mechanism with his left hand.

Gaia was already a blur of motion. Apparently Marsh had aimed his weapon toward Will when Gaia's right foot swung around like a sailboat boom, knocking the gun from his grasp. A split second later she whirled around again, knocking Marsh flat with her left foot.

Will grabbed the knife off the unconscious guard and began sawing through the rest of the bindings.

"Will!" Gaia shouted as she planted her knees on Marsh's chest. "Stop Catherine!"

Catherine? Will's mind chugged sluggishly through his fear and astonishment. *The explosives!*

He finished freeing his other hand and feet and leaped up. Gripping the semiautomatic, he hurried to the rear corner of the bunker, where Catherine was stooped behind a crate. An array of tools lay before her, many of them the same instruments Will remembered using during their bomb-defusing simulations back at Quantico. Her hands clutched a small black resin box swaddled in duct tape.

A remote arming device.

"Catherine," Will said, trying to keep his voice calm and his hand steady as he aimed the barrel of the gun at her head. "Don't do this."

"Sorry. You'll just have to kill me," she said plainly. She picked up a wire cutter and calmly snipped off some copper coils at the base of the unit.

Will swallowed hard. "Put it *down*, Catherine."

"No."

What should he do? As dire as things were, he didn't want to shoot her. Besides, one stray bullet could end up detonating the several pounds of C-4 explosives they had stored around here.

Behind him he could hear Gaia and Marsh still struggling. He had to do something fast. As he raised his weapon to fire, Catherine looked him straight in the eye, lifted the remote unit, and dramatically hit a metal switch. The mechanism let out a harsh electronic buzz that rattled right through Will.

"I just armed all the explosives," Catherine said with a possessed smile. "Don't waste your time trying to disarm them, either. I installed a lock-out device. Any attempts to circumvent it will short-circuit the system and immediately detonate the explosives. And by the time you removed the device, the countdown will have run out. It's foolproof." She seemed so pleased with herself, like an honor roll student bragging about her science fair experiment.

"Good girl," came Marsh's voice behind them.

Will spun around in time to see Marsh's boot slam into his chest. A sharp pain radiated through him and he found himself flying backward. He hit the floor and slid a foot or two, his head banging against the concrete.

His sight grew blurry, and strange lights flickered in his field of vision. Shapes scurried in front of him. Catherine and Marsh. He knew he had to do something, but his body was too seized up with pain to respond.

"She tricked me!" he heard Catherine say, her voice choked with hurt and anger. "I'm so sorry, Dad!"

"Let the bombs finish them," Marsh said. "We have to leave now." Will could see their fuzzy shapes race past him, into the anteroom and up the iron ladder to the tunnel.

He shook his head, trying to jar his senses back. Slowly he managed to pull himself to his knees. Just when he was staggering to his feet, a moan sounded nearby. *Gaia!*

She lay on the floor on the other side of the room, slowly twisting back and forth as if dazed. Will raced to her side. "Gaia! You okay?"

Gaia tried to raise herself up, but with her hands still tied behind her, she only managed to lift her chin slightly. She muttered a string of curse words and then fell flat again. "Marsh fights like a man half his age," she grumbled.

Will carefully helped her to her feet. A box cutter lay on a crate nearby. He picked it up and hurriedly sliced her bindings. "Hold still," he said.

Gaia glanced around the room. "Where's Catherine? Where the hell is Marsh?"

27

"They just got away."

"What? How?" she shrieked, her energy stores apparently restocked.

Will waited a beat, concentrating on cutting the ropes until he'd freed her right hand, then her left. The rest of the bindings fell to the floor in a heap. "When Catherine armed the detonators, I got distracted and Marsh jumped me."

"You mean the explosives are set to go off?" she asked.

"In less than thirty minutes," Will concluded, circling his right shoulder to get the stiffness out.

Gaia's purplish-blue eyes swiveled upward for a moment, then locked back onto his with a newly charged gleam. "You follow Marsh and Catherine," she said. "They must have an escape route planned."

She raced to the sawed-out opening in the room's far wall and threw her legs over the side. A second later he heard her feet clang onto the metal catwalk below.

"Wait a minute! *Wait a minute!*" Will called out, running after her. He got on his knees and poked his head out into the murky darkness. "Where do you think you're going?" he shouted over the sound of rushing water.

"I've got to get back to the courthouse and warn everyone about the explosives," came her muffled voice from below.

"No! You can't go back down there! The detonators are armed, and there may not be enough time!"

But Gaia was already running along the catwalk, her blond hair fading into the gloom.

warn the others

Gaia crept up the rope ladder that Rossiter and the others had left hanging down the shaft of the tunnel. Her legs ached, and she was out of breath from having run all the way down the underground catwalks back to the courthouse. By her estimation, it had taken her almost fifteen minutes to get to this point. That meant she had less than fifteen minutes to warn the others before the explosives went off, risking a full or partial collapse of the building and the countless deaths of innocent people.

She reached the top of the ladder and hoisted herself onto the floor of the courthouse's fallout shelter, stirring up tiny eddies of dust and plaster shavings. Footprints were everywhere in the silty powder—big bootlike treads that could only have come from James Rossiter and his three thugs. She wondered where they were at this moment—if they could have possibly sprung Nino amid all the FBI agents and extra security.

Gaia followed the tracks to the iron rungs that headed straight up a narrow shaft to the building's basement. As she pulled herself onto the grimy vinyl floor, her lungs rejoiced at the far less dirty and oppressive air. After the gloom of the tunnels, it was both surprising and pleasant to see daylight spilling into the room through a high, narrow window.

She had just risen onto her feet when she heard voices floating down the nearby corridor, punctuated by heavy footfalls.

"Damn FBI!" someone was muttering. "All those months of planning and the hearing gets rescheduled."

Gaia instantly recognized the gruff bullfrog voice. It had been ingrained in her mind since their first exchange in Moscone's Diner. It was Rossiter, Socorro's terrorist bomber extraordinaire. And judging by the number of footsteps, she surmised his men were with him. They seemed to be hurrying through the dim basement toward the trapdoor to the bomb shelter.

"I swear I'm going to snap that blond agent's neck like a twig."

Rossiter rounded the corner and found himself face-to-face with Gaia. A look of surprise passed over his hideous mug.

"Hi," she said sweetly before planting the heel of her palm into his nose. Gaia felt the cartilage collapse beneath the force of her blow.

Rossiter let out an anguished yelp and covered his face with his hands. Blood trickled between his fingers, running in stripes down his hairy arms. Gaia took advantage of his debilitated state to wheel her right foot around, crashing it into his kneecap. He crumpled forward, his gun tumbling into the opening of the tunnel.

A second later one of the nameless, fatigue-wearing thugs raced around the corner. But Gaia was ready. She knocked his arm wide with a circular blow, sending his pistol clattering beneath a metal storage cabinet. Then she whirled behind him and followed with a quick strike to the neck. The man fell to his knees, his head lolling. No sooner did he topple forward, unconscious, when Nameless Thugs 2 and 3 came careening into view with their guns drawn.

Gaia elbowed the closest one in the solar plexus while simultaneously kicking the other's gun. As Thug 2 doubled over, gasping, Thug 3 reeled backward, his arms flailing for balance. His right index finger tightened on the trigger, sending a round of machine-gun fire straight into the ceiling.

Fragments of plaster rained down on their heads. Gaia really hoped no one upstairs had been hurt.

She finished off Thug 2 with a fierce uppercut punch to the jaw and then neutralized Thug 3 with a swift kick to the head. She heard the twin thuds of their bodies hitting the floor and then suddenly an earsplitting ringing blared through the walls, vibrating her breastbone.

It was an alarm. Yes! The gunfire must have set it off. With any luck, they would now seal off the building, preventing anyone else from entering.

Now all she had to do was warn everyone inside to get outside

Her triumph was cut short by a sudden, fierce tugging at her feet. She glanced down and saw James Rossiter gripping her ankles with his bloody hands. *You've got to be kidding,* she thought.

"You aren't going anywhere!" he yelled. Blood still gushed from his nose into his mouth, coating his crooked teeth.

She lurched forward, dragging him a few inches until she reached the sprawled form of Thug 3. Reaching beneath him, Gaia yanked Rossiter's machine gun out from under his chest and pointed it right at his grotesque face.

"Either you let me go," she hissed, "or I will splatter your brain matter all over your friends."

Fear bloomed behind his bleary, bloodshot eyes. He released her leg and slowly raised his hands into the air. "You're crazy!" he wheezed.

She grinned ironically. "I'm so going to enjoy this." In two quick motions she rammed him hard in the temple with the butt of the gun and then finished him off with a quick chop to the base of his skull. Rossiter's bulbous eyes rolled back into his head and he collapsed facedown on the floor.

New sounds rent the air. People were shouting, doors were slamming, and feet were tramping down the stairwells. Gaia was just turning toward the approaching noises when the room suddenly began to dip and sway. Her body was starting to get that heavy, droopy feeling, warning her that her adrenaline supply would soon be exhausted.

Not yet! she pleaded as she walked crookedly down the corridor, her vision slowly growing dim.

She blinked hard, forcing herself to stay conscious, but she was losing power rapidly. Two steps later she stumbled forward, sprawling onto her knees. *No! I have to warn the others!*

The sounds of pounding feet and yelling came from a nearby corridor, but they seemed to be growing more distant. Gaia crawled forward, biting her lip, chomping her tongue, doing anything she could think of to keep herself awake. Eventually she turned the corner where the noises seemed to be emanating from. She tried to focus into the distance, but her sight was blurry and growing dim. She could only roll onto her back and watch the ceiling shimmer in and out of focus.

A shout rang out, followed by more footsteps. Suddenly a man in a guard's uniform crouched down beside her.

"Miss? Do you need help?"

Gaia dredged her system for a few final ounces of strength. "Agent Moore . . . FBI," she gasped, fumbling in her pocket for her ID card. "Bombs set to go off . . . Evacuate building . . . right away. . . ."

Her chest felt like it was collapsing, making speech impossible. Gaia fixed the guard with a final, pleading stare before his face dissolved and everything swirled into blackness.

A JOB TO DO

The rusty metal rungs chafed Will's already rope-burned hands as he climbed up the seemingly endless shaft, cursing the entire way. Gaia and her Superwoman complex. Socorro and their perverted schemes. The Philadelphia Water Department and its catacomb-like tunnels.

He didn't want to be brave right now. But he had a job to do. A job any FBI agent should be able to carry out. He had to capture Catherine and Marsh.

And it wasn't necessarily courage that fueled him. It was more like pride. He wanted to make Gaia proud of him. Plus he needed to prove to himself that he was still a tough guy in spite of the fear that had gripped him the past couple of hours. The old Will was in there somewhere; he just had to shake him back into place.

He was nearing the top now, he could tell. Watery light was seeping into the tunnel, and Will could smell the breath of the city: car exhaust mixed with the cool, mossy scent of the Delaware River. Twenty rungs later, he poked his head out into the sunshine.

He was staring down a long, narrow alley shadowed by the high walls of several old, red-and-yellow-brick buildings. One end was blocked by a row of rusted Dumpsters, but the far end was open. And in between ran two lone figures—Catherine and Marsh.

"Stop!" Will called as he heaved himself out of the tunnel and onto the surrounding asphalt. "Stop or I'll shoot!"

The pair slowed long enough to glance back at him. Will heard Marsh say something to Catherine, and the two of them charged forward again.

Holding the gun out in front of him, Will raced toward them, commanding his Olympic-trained legs to propel him as fast as possible. He narrowed the gap by several yards, but it was clear he would never overtake them before the alley ended. In the light beyond he could make out the movement of cars and a few pedestrians.

If they merged into the morning traffic, he might never catch them. And shooting at them on a downtown street, just starting its day, would not be an option.

"Stop or I'll fire!" he shouted again.

They continued running, now only yards away from the end of the alley. He had to do something—and fast.

Will dropped to one knee, took careful aim, and fired his gun. *Blam!* The shot echoed off the high walls of the alley. And Catherine fell to the ground.

"Oh my God," Will muttered. He'd done it. He'd shot her.

He ran forward just as Marsh stopped and turned. Even from a distance Will could see the pain in Marsh's expression. Deep lines rutted his forehead and his mouth was twisted into a painful pucker.

Catherine rolled onto her back, moaning and clutching at her right leg. A dark rivulet of blood glistened beside her. "I'm okay, Dad!" she gasped, tears streaming out of her eyes. "Keep running!"

"No!" Will warned, pointing the pistol at Marsh. He was breathless, and he couldn't feel his fingers anymore, as if a stranger's hand had somehow been grafted onto his arm.

"Don't listen to him!" Catherine choked out. *"Run!"*

Marsh held Will's gaze for a few seconds before he turned and continued fleeing up the alley, disappearing into the sunlight beyond.

"Stop!" Will cried again. His hand with the gun was shaking uncontrollably and sweat trickled down his forehead. *"Stop!"*

"You can't stop him now!" Catherine wheezed joyfully. "He's gone!"

But Will hadn't been talking to Marsh. He'd been talking to himself. *What's wrong with me?* he wondered. *Why couldn't I shoot?*

Just then a low rumble sounded in the distance and the ground shook beneath his feet.

The explosives! Will's heart stopped. Where was Gaia?

Suddenly, losing Marsh didn't seem like such a big deal anymore.

Will

I've always put crazy amounts of pressure on myself. It's like I have this need to prove myself—to my friends, my superiors, even to me. I've pushed to the brink of my own limits my entire life. No big deal. But ever since Gaia told me her huge genetic secret, I've felt a new pressure: to make myself worthy of her.

It's crazy and complicated, and I don't know how to feel my way through it. Gaia's more than strong, more than tough. Almost superhuman. It's not like she looks down on me, but I still can't shake the feeling that I'm less than she is.

I want to be her equal, even . . . dare I say it? . . . her superior. It's stupid and sexist, I know, but I want to be her gallant knight. Just once I'd like to swoop in and save her from harm and then have her look me in the eye and call me her hero. That's part of the reason why I followed her to Socorro's lair and why I blew off my career to meet her in Philadelphia.

I know she sees weakness in me. She protects me, puts herself in jeopardy to save me from harm's way. It's the most emasculating thing imaginable. It should have been me in that blast. Gaia should have been the one running for safety.

I've never liked to lose. And if I lose Gaia, I lose everything.

Will finally found her, lying on an ambulance gurney among the cluster of emergency vehicles parked outside the remains of the courthouse.

"Gaia!" he shouted, pushing past some uniformed police.

She didn't move. A dense weight settled in his chest. Was she still breathing? It was hard to tell at this distance.

He hurried through the crowd, keeping his eyes locked on her motionless, forlorn-looking shape. She was sprawled on her back, with one leg slightly bent outward and one arm drooping to the dusty pavement. Her head was turned toward him, but tufts of her lemony blond hair covered her face. She looked so delicate and slight, not at all like the powerful warrior he knew and worshiped.

"Gaia," he called again as he ran toward the gurney. But before he could reach her side, a man stepped in front of him.

"Can I help you, sir?" he asked in a gruff voice, holding his right hand stiffly out in front of him to halt Will.

"That's my friend," Will said, indicating Gaia with a nod. "My partner."

The man frowned. "Your partner?"

"Yes," Will muttered impatiently, looking past him at Gaia. He reached into his pocket and pulled out his temporary agent status card, slightly bent and cracked from all his recent activities.

The man glanced at it and nodded. "I was with Agent Moore when she collapsed, unconscious," he said. "I'm Agent MacFarland of the Philadelphia division." He flipped open a leather billfold to reveal a real, pristine FBI ID card.

"Is she all right?" Will asked.

Agent MacFarland shook his head. "I'm not sure. But she managed to warn us that the building was coming down. Thanks to her, we got all personnel out safely."

Will's mouth cocked into a sideways grin. That was his girl, all right. She'd done it. She'd warned them in time.

A low moan emanated from the stretcher, and Gaia slowly turned her head back and forth.

"Gaia!" he exclaimed. He turned to Agent MacFarland. "Please. Let me speak with her."

"I'll let you talk while I call my superior." Agent MacFarland stepped aside and pressed a wireless to his ear.

Will leaped toward the gurney. "Gaia? Can you hear me?" He snatched up her hand and held it to his chest, squeezing it tightly.

"Will?" she said weakly, her long lashes fluttering.

"Yeah, it's me." She started to sit up, but he gently held her down by her shoulder, happy to play the role of caretaker. "Whoa. Easy now. You need to rest."

"What happened to Catherine and Marsh?" she asked, her eyes darting around.

"They just took Catherine away in an ambulance. I shot her, Gaia. I had to." His voice seemed to catch on something and he paused to clear his throat. "They think she's going to be okay, though."

"You did what you had to," she said, studying him. Her hand gave his a tiny squeeze. "What about Marsh?"

"He . . . got away," Will mumbled, hoping the guilt wasn't too evident in his expression. No need to tell her, or anyone else for that matter, the real story. As far as the world was concerned,

Marsh had slipped into the crowd on the street before Will got a chance to shoot.

"Damn," Gaia muttered, closing her eyes.

"Don't worry," Will said. "They've got people looking everywhere. They'll find him."

"No, they won't," Gaia grumbled. "He's too smart."

Will winced at the implication of her words.

"Sir?" Agent McFarland walked toward them, clicking his cell phone shut. "I've just been on the phone with my division heads. They want to thank you and Agent Moore for all of your help. Thanks to you, we managed to save a lot of lives and we still have Nino in custody."

"Our pleasure," Will said, feeling himself puff up a little.

"And there's one other thing," Agent MacFarland added, his face folding into a worried expression.

"What's that?"

"I'm supposed to take the two of you into custody."

every tiny movement

Conan O'Brien was talking. His lips were moving, and his eyebrows were doing that wiggle thing. Meanwhile, an unseen audience laughed hysterically.

It was clear Conan was on fire tonight, not that Gaia could appreciate it. She tried to follow his monologue, but after three or four words her mind would mosey away to the shabby room's brown wool drapes or cheesy leaf-patterned bedspread.

After an endless afternoon of questions from FBI, court officials, and local police, they'd been released, provided with a rental car (Catherine's Altima had been impounded), and ordered back to their base to face disciplinary action. Gaia was pleased they were trusted enough to drive themselves. They decided to stay at a motel and drive the three hours in the morning. It would give them a chance to rest up so they could be at their best when they faced Malloy and Bishop the next day.

The only motel they could find had just one room to spare. So there she was, sitting beside Will on an old, saggy mattress. Yet another ugly motel room in this long, screwed-up adventure.

Conan made a crack about his hair and mugged for the camera. The audience roared, but Gaia couldn't even force a smile. Beside her, Will seemed just as disinterested. He hadn't laughed once since the show began, and from what she could tell, his gaze was also meandering about the room.

"You sleepy?" Gaia asked.

"No," he replied. "I'm really tired. Just not sleepy."

"Yeah," she said, nodding. She knew just what he meant. Her body felt like it had been pushed through a mulcher, but for some reason, her brain just wouldn't shut down. Her thoughts kept leapfrogging over each other, making it impossible to follow a single thread. Well . . . except one: she was constantly aware that she was sitting next to Will on a king-sized bed in the middle of nowhere.

Gaia had never been so hyperconscious of someone's presence. She was noticing every tiny movement of his, every flick of a finger or shift in his weight. She even wondered if he had a few bruised ribs, because his breathing seemed rapid and shallow. And she could practically see his body heat emanating off him. It made her feel cold somehow, and she found herself wanting—no, almost *needing*—him to put his arms around her.

Since she'd woken up on the stretcher, he'd been staring at her with the same weighed-down expression—as if he didn't want to let her out of his sight. Fear did such a number on people, even the really tough ones like Will. Pouncing on him right now might just spook him even more.

A commercial came on, featuring a toothy model smiling at a bottle of mouthwash. The woman swished the liquid around in her mouth, still smiling the entire time as if it was the most fun she'd ever had. Then suddenly the scene changed to show her walking along the street, where an equally toothsome male appeared out of nowhere and started kissing her.

Gaia squirmed against the headboard, feeling an intense rush of nostalgia. Less than twenty-four hours before, she and Will had been kissing the exact same way, fulfilling the destiny that had seemed obvious ever since the first time they'd laid eyes on each other at the Quantico training course. No. Not the same. Their kiss had been better. Closer.

She ached to return to it. After so many days of not-right feelings, it had been the only thing that felt right. She had just told Will about her fearlessness when it happened—the first and only time she'd divulged her secret to anyone. And instead of driving him away, it had brought him closer, leading to the most intensely intimate moment of her life.

Now Gaia found herself pining for that moment, wanting to tap into its power. But she had no idea how.

So she sat and listened to Will breathe, waiting for a sign.

After a couple more commercials, Will suddenly stretched out his arms and let out a weary sigh. "You want to keep watching this?" he asked.

Gaia shrugged. "I don't care. Do you?"

"Not really." He hit the remote and the TV powered off, enveloping them in darkness.

Gaia leaned over, reaching toward the lamp on the nearby nightstand. She clicked it on and a bright yellowish light filled the room.

"Jeez!" she exclaimed, squinting. "What's the wattage on this bulb? Supernova?" She pulled her arm back and then winced in sudden pain.

Will noticed. "What's wrong?" he asked.

"Nothing."

"Don't give me that. You're hurt."

"I've got a knot in my shoulder muscle. No big deal." She tried to shrug and flinched again.

Will regarded her distrustfully. "If *you're* registering pain, it's a big deal. Come on. Let me see."

Gaia let out a frustrated grunt and pointed to a spot just below her left shoulder. "There, see? I just wrenched it, that's all. The damn super-soldiers tied me too tight."

"You should let me rub out the kinks. Otherwise you'll be in real pain tomorrow." Will touched the area with his fingertips.

Gaia let out a small moan. It felt like warm electrical currents were trilling through her body. "Okay," she mumbled, giving in. "Thanks."

His fingers gingerly searched her side. "Could you, um, lift your shirt? I really can't reach the spot with your sleeve in the way."

Gaia raised herself up and lifted her top so that her entire back was exposed. "How's that?" she asked, lying on her stomach.

There came a slight pause. "Uh . . . good. Thanks."

"Press down hard, okay?" she murmured, her voice half muffled by the pillow. "I can take it."

Will's hands dug into the sore spot and a searing pain shot through her body.

"Ow!" she cried, going rigid.

"You said to press hard."

"Yeah, but not *that* hard!" Gaia smiled into the pillow. If nothing else, they might at least have a good fight tonight. Then maybe she could get some sleep.

Will glanced down at Gaia's bare, sloping back. The glow of the nearby lamp illuminated her skin and ignited the gold in her hair.

Without thinking, Will stopped kneading her muscles and began stroking his hands down the length of her back, from her shoulders to the gentle dip above the top of her jeans. Her skin was so smooth, so unlike the tough-as-ground-glass attitude she projected. She was much softer than she seemed.

Gaia let out a small humming sound and shifted slightly. She seemed to like his lighter touch. Feeling emboldened, he continued sliding his fingers along her back and sides.

His twitchy nervousness was gone. Everything seemed to be in place. This was where he was supposed to be. With Gaia. Here. Doing this. He knew it with every burning molecule in his body.

As he continued rubbing her velvety skin, a giddy feeling slowly came over him. The lamplight was so bright, her body was so warm, and the air practically crackled all around them. The room seemed suddenly radioactive. Hypnotized, he pushed her hair off to one side, leaned forward, and began kissing the curve of her neck.

Gaia rolled over, and for a long moment they simply met each other's gaze, smiling faintly. Her hands slipped beneath his T-shirt and traveled up and down the length of his torso, leaving a crop of goose bumps in their wake. A heavy, tingly sensation trilled through his limbs. He grabbed the bottom edge of his shirt and yanked it up and over his head, letting it fall to the carpet. Then hers.

Will and Gaia exchanged another fleeting grin, and then he found himself falling forward, descending into her gravity until their lips met. They kissed deeply, their bodies reshifting to settle into each other's contours and crevices. When they broke off, her mouth instantly curled into an impish grin.

Somewhere down in the cellar of his mind he wondered how she could kiss and smile at the same time. But he didn't allow the thought out. He couldn't greet any thoughts except Gaia. He dipped forward toward her again.

Gaia quivered beneath him, her fingers digging into his scalp. As he sat back against her legs and began unbuttoning her jeans, his eyes met hers, searching for any hesitation. But there was none. She allowed him to be the aggressor. Her face looked serene, free of the usual burdens that constantly weighed down her delicate features.

Will felt a surge of . . . what? Desire, yes. But something more. Honor. That was it. He felt honored to be holding this majestic creature. This woman. This force in his life.

His heart put on a burst of speed, accelerating his breath and movements. Their kiss deepened, zippers were yanked open, and two pairs of jeans hit the floor.

And Will became lost in a rush of sensations.

Gaia

This is really happening.

Will and I about to become Willandl.

A tiny cool spot in my brain is shouting through the frenzied emotions, asking me to stop and think about this for a minute. But it's hard to think. All I can do right now is feel.

I'm never "afraid" of consequences. I've learned to exercise a level of self-discipline usually reserved for Zen Buddhist masters or victims of obsessive-compulsive disorder. I know the logical ramifications of someone like me losing control would be magnified times two hundred. So while growing up, I rarely let myself give in to my yearnings. (Unless my yearning was to pummel a would-be mugger into a quivering glob.)

But I'm tired of being super-rigid self-control girl. I want to drop my defenses and surrender everything for a change. My secrets, my past, my future . . . my everything. I'm tired of dwelling on the past and overanalyzing the future. I want to live in the now.

And right now I want him.

A REAL POTENTIAL

Gaia woke up to the orange liquid light of morning streaming in through the crack in the brown polyester drapes. She yawned and arched her back while stretching her toes as far as they could go.

Will was asleep beside her. They lay clutching each other, their limbs woven together, her head resting in the crook above his right shoulder. In the tangle of body parts it was impossible to tell which arm or leg belonged to whom.

She lay completely still, taking in every tiny sensation. The gleam of sunlight against Will's skin. The warm breeze of his breath wafting across her neck. The rumbling of cardiac activity vibrating their chests.

Will took a deep breath. His chest lifted Gaia's head, and a patch of whiskers on his chin brushed against her cheek. Eventually his lashes fluttered and opened. His ice blue eyes focused and fixed directly on her.

"Morning," she greeted with a smile.

"Hey," he said, his voice husky with sleep. He sat up and blinked around at the shabby hotel room, as if he wasn't sure where he was.

She watched as he quickly slid out of bed and picked through the pile of clothes for his boxers. Scenes from the night before replayed in her mind. Her skin tingled as she remembered the shuddery excitement, the sharp, earthy scents of Will's body, the warmth and sweat. She couldn't remember the last time she'd felt so free and happy.

Will pulled on his shorts and sank into a nearby chair. "What time is it?" he mumbled, rubbing his eyes. "We've got to get on the road."

"Almost eight thirty," Gaia replied, glancing at the digital clock on the nightstand. They'd have to answer for their actions this morning, in front of a panel of their superiors. There was a real possibility they would be dismissed because of the choices they had made. She sat up and crossed her arms over her chest, hugging herself. The room felt suddenly cold without Will holding her. She slipped out of bed and rummaged about for her clothes.

"Do you want to shower first?" she asked, pulling on her underwear.

He was still watching her closely. "Yeah. No. I don't know," he muttered. "Do you?"

She shook her head as she poked it through the opening in her shirt. "You go first. I'd give good money for a toothbrush, though."

The barest of smiles breezed across Will's face and disappeared. He drummed his palms against his knees and glanced around the room, as if the bathroom was difficult to find. He let out a sigh as he rose to his feet and crossed the room. He ran his hand through his blond bristles and reached for a towel before closing the door.

Will obviously had a lot on his mind. As did she. Like, could they still be partners after this? (Assuming, of course, that Malloy and Bishop let them stay.) Could they still deal with each other on a professional level? Did last night actually mean something, or was it some cathartic reaction to the cutthroat-rivalry-meets-sexual-tension that existed between them?

But Gaia didn't want to think about that right now. She couldn't think at all. Her mind was shutting down, save for the flashes of memory that continued like a slide show behind her eyes. She closed them so that she could pay full attention to the show.

It was the only thing that felt right.

". . . absent without leave from a government training facility, defying the orders of a superior, attacking bureau personnel . . ."

Gaia's gaze traveled from Special Agent Malloy's ruddy, pockmarked face to Agent Bishop's blank, placid expression, to the swirly pattern in the wood grain of the desk.

Meanwhile, Malloy continued rattling off their long list of violations. At the time she'd committed said atrocities, she'd been on such a mad, obsessive quest to help her partner and roommate that it had been easy to rationalize her actions. She'd done everything out of loyalty to her friend and her intense frustration with a system that treated Catherine's disappearance as a statistic.

Of course, Catherine had ended up being an undercover plant for a terrorist cell, which sort of dampened the whole noble savior aspect of the mission.

Malloy was still going. ". . . misuse of FBI equipment and personnel—yes, we are aware of Lyle's involvement—trespassing, breaking and entering . . ."

Gaia turned her head ever so slightly in order to get a better peripheral view of Will as he stood beside her. She could tell by his overly erect posture and rigid jaw that he was afraid but unwilling to show it. The final leg of their drive back to Quantico had been painfully silent, rife with post-sex awkwardness and the realization that they were most likely heading toward their occupational demises.

Gaia wondered if Bishop and Malloy had picked up the shift in her and Will's relationship. To her it seemed like it should be glaringly obvious. As much as they tried to appear professional, anyone could see that the measure of personal space between them had narrowed. And at times, as Malloy blustered on, Gaia's disobedient mind would detach itself from the present and jump back to the previous night, reliving the heat and passion and sweaty desperation. But just when her skin warmed to the point where it felt like it might slide off, Gaia would wrench her mind back on track.

She stole another look at Will, resisting the overwhelming urge to grab his hand.

I'll save him, she told herself. *As soon as they officially can us, I'll convince them that Will had little to do with it—that I forced him somehow. Then they'll have to reconsider letting him go.*

"... and most egregious of all, you shifted your focus away from the trail of the lollipop murderer." Malloy closed the file he'd been reading from and set it on his desk with palatable disgust.

Gaia shuddered as a sudden wave of nausea washed over her. She hadn't given a thought to the string of brutal murders since defecting to find Catherine. Her lack of focus and commitment to her assignment could potentially cost someone else her life. It was a sobering thought.

Agent Bishop stepped up to the desk. "Let's move straight to the outcome of this matter."

Gaia frowned. During her months with the FBI, Bishop and Malloy had often put up a good-cop, bad-cop front with them. She had expected the same here. But while Malloy was definitely playing his brusque part (she couldn't imagine him any other way), Bishop wasn't exactly exuding warmth and understanding. In fact, she seemed almost starchy.

Could this be worse than Gaia had previously thought? Instead of just getting thrown out of Quantico, was it possible the marine outside the door would march them off to the brig?

"Malloy and I have discussed these events with our superiors," Agent Bishop resumed, "and have concluded that your simulation training here at Quantico has come to an end."

There. She'd said it. Both Gaia and Will instinctively bowed their heads. Gaia had thought she was prepared for this expected result. But each of Agent Bishop's crisply delivered words burrowed inside her like barbed wire. Gaia pulled out her badge and set it on the desk beside her fat personnel file.

"You misunderstand me," Bishop said, looking at Gaia. "I meant that both of you have concluded this phase of your training and will now be given rookie status."

Gaia froze, her gun harness half unbuckled. Out of the corner of her eye she could see Will perk up in surprise.

"Beg your pardon?" he said.

"Don't misunderstand," Bishop continued. "While we feel you have completed the necessary training, you still face disciplinary charges for leaving the base without consent. Your comings and goings from this campus will be monitored very closely, and each of you will meet with our staff psychiatrist to ensure you are still fit for duty."

"But we had psych evaluations when we were recruited," Will pointed out.

"That is correct, Agent Taylor. However, routine evaluations are given throughout an agent's career and are mandatory after stressful field situations. Both you and Agent Moore have experienced potentially traumatic events in the past couple of days. You will meet with Dr. Lehman tomorrow. Understood?"

"Yes, ma'am," Gaia and Will said in unison.

Bishop turned toward Gaia. "Agent Moore? Does this look familiar?" He held up a clear evidence bag. Inside was a handheld tape recorder.

"My log!" Gaia exclaimed as she recognized the telltale smear of ketchup on its black casing. She'd thought she'd never see it again.

Malloy nodded. "We know. We've listened."

"It was"—Bishop pursed her lips, as if searching for the right word—"enlightening."

"A transcript of your entries will be included in your file, along with the report detailing your disobedience and abuses of power," Malloy went on. "Your file will also include a copy of a letter, faxed this morning from Judge Constance Massey, who has been overseeing the Ramon Nino case. Here is a copy for your own records." She handed Gaia a sheet of paper with an official government logo at the top.

A warm sense of pride seeped through Gaia as she skimmed the neatly typed page. "'The city of Philadelphia and the United States Government are indebted to FBI agent trainee Gaia Moore. . . . prevented incalculable number of casualties . . . risked her life to warn building security . . .'" She tried not to smile as she folded the paper in half and returned to her at-attention stance. *Someone noticed,* she cheered inwardly. *After years of anonymous butt kicking and ass saving, someone finally cared enough to say thank you.*

Malloy leaned forward across his desk. "While we might

understand your reluctance to work with the bureau on this matter, that doesn't excuse it. Although you showed good instinct in having Agent Taylor check out Marsh, you allowed a wanted criminal to turn you completely against your own organization. This is a huge warning flag on your record. The fact that you put things right doesn't fully erase it. You will have to earn our trust all over again, Agent Moore. As will you, Agent Taylor," he added turning toward Will.

"Thank you," Gaia said, meeting Agent Bishop's eyes, then Malloy's. "We won't let you down again."

"Right," Will chimed in. "We won't."

Malloy and Bishop nodded back at them, unsmiling.

"One more thing," Malloy said, resting his thick, callused hands on the tabletop. "As another consequence of your actions, you will no longer be allowed to partner on any cases. Agent Taylor, you will be put on research and administrative duties until we place you with a mentor partner. Agent Moore, you will resume your investigation into the Lollipop Murder Case with Agent Lau. Is that understood?"

For the first time since they'd entered the office, Gaia and Will looked at each other. She could see him tense up—his chest heaved with faster and shallower breaths and his hands tightened reflexively.

They do *know about us.* That had to be it. She knew things were going too well to be true.

Will turned back to their superiors. "I don't understand," he said in a slow, measured voice. "I'm being taken off the case . . . why?"

"We don't feel you and Agent Moore have the right working dynamic. You are both too similar—excellent instincts but rather lax on protocol," Agent Bishop replied. "On the other hand, although Agent Lau did break several rules by helping you to track down Moore, he also showed a great regard for FBI regulations by coming forward and cooperating in our efforts to find you." She paused for a moment and stared at each of them, her eyebrows disappearing behind her pageboy bangs. "Is this going to be a problem?"

Gaia stood stock-still as she considered this. After everything she and Will had been through together recently, it didn't seem right to split them up. Their adventure had drawn them together, deepened their understanding of each other, and increased the sense of loyalty and trust between them. And they were both equally committed to bringing down the culprit in the Lollipop Murders.

On the other hand, maybe they'd grown too close. The tryst in the motel had been a blissful break in a series of horrifying events. But as much as she'd needed it, she had to admit it also posed some important questions. Like . . . what now? Could they actually spend long hours together on a case without giving in to temptations? Plus she and Will really were a lot alike—they'd even discussed it themselves. Disagreements tended to blow up into full-scale battles. And agreements? They occasionally escalated into something very different but just as distracting.

The Lollipop Case needed to be investigated thoroughly and professionally, with no delays and no room for errors. All those poor women who'd been viciously killed, all those young boys who'd been orphaned—they deserved justice.

On this matter, Gaia had to choose the case over Will. She just hoped he understood.

"No, Agent Bishop," Gaia replied, looking her superior in the eye. "There's no problem."

"Good." Agent Bishop glanced over at Malloy, as if giving him a signal.

"Very well, then." Malloy pushed back his high-back leather chair and settled into it. "In that case, you are both dismissed."

Gaia felt a loosening sensation, as if an invisible strap that had been holding her in place had suddenly snapped, allowing her to more freely move and breathe. She turned toward Will, hoping to flash him a bolstering look, but he was already bolting through the doorway.

"Agent Moore," Malloy called out just as Gaia made to follow him.

"Yes, sir?" Gaia spun around, willing her eyes not to stare longingly toward the exit.

"Don't forget that I'll need a full report from you by tomorrow. I want to know everything that happened, from the time you left this base to the time you returned. Is that clear?"

"Uh . . . yes, sir."

She turned and headed into the corridor, her mind spinning with a spanking-new concern. Did Malloy really need to know *everything*?

HIDDEN CLUES

After leaving the chief's office, Gaia searched the corridor for Will. He wasn't there. Nor was he by the elevators or in the reception area on the first floor. He hadn't waited for her at all.

He's pissed. She didn't blame him for being mad about getting booted off the Lollipop Case. But he wasn't mad at *her*, was he?

She finally spotted him walking through the quadrangle. His stride was long, quick, and purposeful, and Gaia had to jog to catch up with him.

"Will! Wait up!" she called, feeling rather silly and slightly annoyed at having to chase him down.

Will stopped walking, his body growing rigid before he slowly turned to face her. "Hey," he said as she came to a stop beside him. His face was an expressionless mask.

"Are you . . . okay?" she asked, searching his eyes for any hidden clues. It was such a nonsense thing to say. So clichéd and vague and grade school–ish. But she didn't want to presume anything on the off chance she'd misunderstood his reaction.

"I'm fine," he said tonelessly. He wouldn't look at her. Instead his eyes focused on an area just past her.

Clearly he was *not* fine.

"I'm sorry they took you off the case," she said, leaning sideways to meet his stare head-on. "I didn't know what to say. I had no choice."

He glanced from her right eye to her left before lowering his gaze to the ground. "I get it," he muttered. "They'd already made up their minds. You couldn't question your superiors."

"Exactly." She felt a rush of relief.

"Of course, you didn't have to take the news so well either," he added.

"What does that mean?" Gaia could feel herself filling with the same rattling frustration she'd become so accustomed to feeling when dealing with Will.

He let out his breath, and his square-backed posture crumpled slightly. "Nothing," he said, against staring past her into the distance. "Just . . . nothing."

Gaia's brow puckered. He was mad at her. And why shouldn't he be? She'd pulled him into the mess with her many secret requests for help, and his reward for helping her was unglamorous desk duty. For someone like Will, it was the worst imaginable punishment.

He shut his eyes and took a deep breath. "Look. I'm still stiff from the drive. All I want to do is work out, shower, and change."

"But we should talk about this. You're upset. I can tell." Why wouldn't he just admit it? Why did he have to fall back into macho mode? She needed to put things right—to make sure he didn't blame her.

"Gaia! Will you stop? I won't lie to you. I'm not exactly thrilled that I've been pulled off the case, but I'm a big boy. I don't need you fussing over me right now!"

She nodded. She was pushing him, demanding that he communicate. It drove her loony whenever someone did that to her, so she could imagine how he felt. After all, they were very much alike—as Malloy and Bishop noted.

So she'd give him some space.

"You're right," she said. "Sorry. I just want to make sure everything's okay between us."

"Everything's fine." He looked over both shoulders and leaned forward, giving her a perfunctory kiss on the forehead. *The forehead?* "I'll see you soon, okay?" he murmured.

"Okay."

Gaia watched him lope off toward the dormitories. His head

was bowed slightly, and his trademark swagger seemed somewhat diminished.

Just a few hours before, they had been holding each other, whispering urgent, passionate phrases. The chemistry between them had been so amazing. They'd been able to read each other so perfectly, fully communicate without speaking.

But not now. As they spoke on the quad, Gaia could almost see a wall being erected between them. He was reverting back to the old Will with his defensive default setting of a stiff jaw, aloof with attitude, and well-timed verbal jabs.

If only she were better at this relationship stuff, with more experience at tackling these little setbacks. But all of her past relationships had ended sadly—usually due to some fault of her own.

She just hoped whatever it was blossoming between her and Will had the strength to survive this.

READY TO RAT

White walls. Not eggshell or cream—just a blah, soul-sapping *white* white. Kim tossed his hand towel over his shoulder and pushed through the metal door of the stairwell. He was so tired of the bland interiors of the Quantico complex buildings that he actually felt a new sympathy toward graffiti artists. How he longed for a tasteful blue. Or mint green. Even a warm beige. He wanted framed original artwork, ornate fixtures, and sisal rugs that cushioned your feet like plush animal fur. What he needed was style and beauty. Because right now, he felt just as empty and weak as the surrounding decor.

Ever since he spilled his guts to Malloy and Bishop about Will, he'd felt depleted of key energy and focus. He knew, logically, that he'd done the right thing—possibly even helped save lives. But he couldn't entirely shake the notion that he had betrayed his friends.

Kim paused just outside the weight room and knelt down to tie the laces on his Reebok trainers. This would be his third workout in as many days. Lately, brisk, cardiovascular exercise was the only thing that cleared his mind and gave him peace, if only for a few breathless moments.

Pushing through the glass door of the weight room, Kim immediately caught sight of an expansive, muscular back and blond square haircut on someone doing shoulder presses.

"Will?"

The back and head turned to reveal Will's face, dripping with sweat.

"Aw, man!" Kim rushed forward, clapping his hand on Will's nearest shoulder.

He'd known they would be returning sometime that day, but that was pretty much the extent of what he'd been told. *At least they're alive,* he kept telling himself. If owning up to his part in Will and Gaia's rogue misdeeds had helped protect them, then it was worth it.

"Where's Gaia? Have you guys already seen Malloy? What's going on? What are they doing to Catherine?" Since the briefing that morning, he'd been trying to get information about the three of them, with no luck. Having helped Will gain access to top secret files, he was now solidly out of the information loop.

As he waited for answers, Kim slowly realized Will wasn't reacting all that warmly. In fact, he wasn't really reacting at all.

Kim's smile faded. "Is everything okay? They didn't kick you guys out, did they?"

Will grinned tightly. "No. We have our rookie status back. Probationary, though."

"That's great news!" Kim broke out laughing and gave him a light shove. "I thought something terrible had happened."

"No, no. Things are great . . ." Will said, his mouth twisting into a sideways smirk. "For *you*."

Kim frowned. "What are you talking about?"

"Come on. Fess up. You went tattling to Malloy about us because you knew they'd reward you somehow."

Will's jaw was set and his broad, beefy chest was puffed up in a gladiator battle stance. But his eyes were weary and sad looking, darting back and forth as if on the run from something. *He's hurt,* Kim told himself.

"That's not true." Kim kept his voice low and controlled. "I did it to keep you guys safe."

"Right. Good ol' reliable, loyal Agent Lau. Ready to rat on his friends in order to help them. And now you got me tossed off the Lollipop Case. Bravo, Lau. Well played."

Will was taken off the Lollipop Case? Why?

Kim stared into his stony expression. Over the weeks he'd seen Will in all types of high-pressure situations, but he'd never seen him like this. His voice was hard and bitter, almost arctic in tone. And there was absolutely no trace of his easygoing spirit. He almost seemed a different person entirely.

"I didn't know they'd do that," Kim said weakly. "You've got to believe me."

Suddenly Will's trademark high-wattage grin returned,

illuminating his features. "Aw, I'm just playing around. Can't you take a joke?"

He punched Kim on the shoulder. Only it wasn't a good-natured, teasing sort of punch—it was a real, knuckles-bruising-skin kind of blow. Not hard enough to knock Kim over or alarm anyone who might be watching, but definitely hard enough to release some pent-up, testosterone-spiked aggression.

Kim's pulse accelerated, and he felt a sudden rush of blood to his face and fists. He resisted his urge to hit Will back.

"I'm just tired, I guess," he said, meeting Will's gaze. "Been a long day."

"I can imagine." Will nodded dramatically. "Probably have that Lollipop Case about solved already, eh?"

Kim frowned. Will had that wide grin on his face, but his teasing was too loaded and perfectly targeted to be in good sport.

Kim had known from day one that Will had come into the FBI to be a superstar. And now this. Getting taken off the case probably ripped him up pretty badly. Kim could feel the pity weighing down his eyes as he looked at Will. It was absolute worst reaction he could give him.

Once again all the light drained from Will's face. "I think I'm done here," he said in a low grumble. "Excuse me while I go hit the showers."

"Will . . ." Kim hastily ducked his head, trying to erase all traces of sympathy from his expression. *Just defer. Make him feel like he's still the alpha male.*

But it was too late. Will was already stalking past him, crashing into Kim's shoulder as he went.

Kim considered apologizing. To someone like Will, pride was

everything. Damaging it was worse than wounding him physically. But it wouldn't do any good. He could only hope that deep down, Will knew the truth: that Kim had truly acted as a loyal friend and ally.

"Glad you guys are safe," he called out.

Will gave no sign of having heard him. Kim watched as his friend pushed through the glass door and disappeared around the corner.

VAGUE TRUTHS

The heavy oak door to Johnny Ray's bar gave a lackluster moan as Gaia pushed it open. Almost instantly the warmth of the room coiled around her. It wasn't a snug warmth but a stifling, sweltering one—full of body heat, cigarette smoke, and the air of desperation.

She shuffled over to the bar, aware of the curious stares directed at her. Although she'd only been in Quantico a short time, she was already a sort of local celebrity. Not exactly the kind that was fawned over, though. Instead, her presence seemed to make people sit up straighter and mind what they said. And that was fine with her. The townies and other recruits were welcome to think of her as that crazy blond chick who liked to punch out guys—especially if it meant she could have a beer in peace.

Little did they know she wasn't that girl anymore. Time, grueling training sessions, and a few hard life lessons had made her better appreciate the presence of people—sane, rational people, that was. And tonight she didn't want to be alone.

The whole community factor was exactly why she was here

instead of in her empty dorm room, which might as well have rubber walls and an echo for all the coziness it provided. Will hadn't been in his room all day or at least hadn't answered when she knocked. Nor had he come by her place or called or left any sort of message. But then . . . by *not* leaving a message he was essentially leaving one. He was telling her that he needed space, that he was still upset about getting taken off the Lollipop Case.

And as irritating as it was, she could grit her teeth and accept it. After all, adding distance was her signature way of dealing with problems, too. Or at least, it had been.

"Hey, there!"

A female voice with a heavy southern twang jolted Gaia from her thoughts. She glanced up to find Kelly, Johnny Ray's owner, rounding the corner of the long, polished wood bar. Her right hand held aloft a circular brown tray piled high with empty beer mugs and red plastic french fry baskets. With her left hand she reached out and patted Gaia's shoulder.

"How are you? I haven't seen you in ages. Been busy?"

"Sort of," Gaia replied.

"Well? Whatcha been up to?"

Oh, you know. Going rogue, eluding an FBI manhunt, finding my "dead" roommate, foiling a terrorist plot, and then having sex with a guy who won't speak with me right now. "Nothing much." She tried to mirror Kelly's wide smile, but it made her cheeks ache.

"Uh-huh?" Kelly's left eyebrow curved with skepticism. Gaia opened her mouth to protest, but Kelly cut her off. "Just sit tight. Let me get rid of this stuff and I'll be right back."

Gaia watched Kelly trot through a doorway behind the bar. *I should go,* she told herself as she began folding a square napkin into halves, then fourths, then eighths. She should just go back to her room and avoid everyone right now. The fact that Kelly had seen right through her made her uneasy.

But as she sat there, waiting for Kelly to reemerge from the back room, Gaia reminded herself that this was exactly why she had come. She needed to unburden herself a little, and Kelly was the closest thing she had to a girlfriend right now. Plus she seemed savvy when it came to people—way more savvy than Gaia. And she was much less intimidating than Kim, who looked deep into your eyes and figured out all your secrets.

She would have never done this before. Five years ago she would have purged her frustration by strolling through a New York City park and pummeling every mugger, drug pusher, and would-be rapist who dared cross her path. But she couldn't do that now that she was a legitimate crime fighter. She was New Gaia. More restrained, but just as tough. And just as lost when it came to sorting out her social life.

Kelly came back through the bright doorway and made a bee-line for Gaia. Her trademark welcoming smile was gone, replaced by a muted but equally friendly half grin. "What are you drinking?" she asked Gaia.

"Beer on tap."

"Coming right up." Kelly moved to the center of the long wooden bar and filled a mug with a frothy amber brew. "Here you go," she said, setting down a fresh square napkin in front of Gaia and placing the mug on top of it. "So what's going on?"

Gaia stared into her sympathetic eyes and felt a strong urge to offer up all of her problems and let herself be mothered by Kelly. But she knew she had to be careful. She couldn't mention anything that was FBI-related or she'd risk jeopardizing her already fragile career.

Kelly leaned forward and rested her arms on the bar between them. "Don't tell me. Guy problems?"

Gaia blinked back at her in surprise. "Well, yeah. At least partially. How did you know?"

"Honey, my whole life is about guy problems. That's why I'm Internet dating!" She gave Gaia a bolstering smile, adding tiny starbursts to the corners of her wide blue eyes. "So does this concern that cute fellow Will, by any chance?"

Gaia stared down at the foam in her beer and nodded. "Partially," she said again. "We really bonded over our latest case. Only now . . . *things* have happened that make everything awkward between us."

"*Things*, huh?" Kelly slouched forward and rested her chin on her right hand with a knowing smile. "So, who's mad at who?"

Gaia hesitated a moment. She wasn't sure she wanted to get this detailed. Yet Kelly was making this sort of easier than she'd expected. "He's mad at me," she replied. "At least I think so." Should she attempt to explain the whole sordid mess? The competitiveness? The fact that Will was the first guy she'd been able to get close to in years? No. It would be too impossible—not to mention potentially painful. Better to stick with vague truths. Baby steps to mental health. "The thing is, I can't really get a straight answer from him."

"Of course not, Gaia. He's a *guy*. Not only can they not talk about their feelings, I'm convinced they can't identify most of them."

Gaia smiled weakly. "Maybe. But I'm still not sure how to

handle it. Do I just leave him alone, or do I go proactive and prove my loyalty to him somehow? What would you do?"

"Oh, hell, sugar. I've made every mistake there is." She shook her head, staring past Gaia toward the empty dance floor. "When I was married, I figured everything that went wrong was my fault, and I would agonize all the time about how to make it right. Terrell, my ex, would blame me for everything he could. He'd even say it was my fault he hit me."

Gaia's hands instinctively closed into fists. "What an asshole."

"Now, now. Don't you go all Wonder Woman on me." Kelly patted Gaia's arm reassuringly. "The point is that I wised up before it was too late. I realized I don't own his problems. It was Jasmine who made me see that."

"Jasmine?" Gaia frowned. Wasn't Jasmine, like, two? "How?"

Kelly's expression dimmed. "Poor little girl started apologizing for things that weren't her fault. Like when Terrell and I had a fight or when he threw things and broke them. One day I realized . . . she learned that from me." A dense weight crept across Kelly's face. "She was so little."

"I'm sorry." Gaia felt a sudden urge to hug Kelly. She'd always sensed there was something wounded about her in spite of her constantly chipper disposition.

"Hey, now." Kelly shook her head briskly, casting off the heavy memory that burdened her features. A peppy sparkle re-ignited her eyes. "This is about you, not me. What I'm trying to say is that this might not be your problem to solve. What point are you guys at anyway? Are you and Will an official couple?"

"I guess so. . . . Not really, though. No." *Good going, Gaia. In five minutes you've gone from vague truths to not making any sense*

*at all. This new opening-up policy is working out quite well. Really
healthy.*

Gaia took a breath and faced her new friend. She could do
this. All she had to do was put forward a little more effort. "I just
feel sort of handicapped when it comes to relationships." *Much
better.* "I hate all the unspoken rules and expectations. Sometimes
I just want to give up and run screaming into the woods." *Oo-kay.
Tone down the raging lunatic bit and you might be on your way to
some emotional stability.*

Kelly rolled her eyes. "Tell me about it. I feel like most guys I
date have these gigantic yet fragile egos that surround them like
eggshells. I've got to watch what I say and do all the time." She
sighed loudly and rested her chin on her hand. "Since my divorce
I've been real careful to screen who I date and not to look for
some knight in shining armor. I can take care of myself now. And
ironically, it's my independence that seems to chase most guys
away. I guess they don't like their women too strong."

Gaia snorted. "I know what you mean." She felt immensely
better.

Kelly stood up straight and smiled. "Speaking of strong
women, I have sort of a big favor to ask of you."

"Anything. Just name it." Gaia could feel her supercharged
adrenaline bubbling up inside her. A taste of her old medicine. What
would it be? Put the fear of God into one of Johnny Ray's overly
amorous regulars? Rough up that slimeball ex-husband of hers?

"Are you sure?" Kelly bit her lower lip. "It's kind of a lot to ask."

"Sure, I'm sure. Just ask."

"Well, okay, then." Kelly smiled in relief. "Gaia? Would you
by any chance be available to babysit for me tomorrow morning?"

Kelly

You meet a lot of characters working in a bar. Loudmouthed truckers, pampered college kids, even an occasional sad case who, after three beers, claims he can pick up signals from Saturn. But Gaia Moore is one of the most intriguing creatures I've ever come across in my, ahem, so many years on the job.

When I see Gaia, it's like looking into a fun-house mirror. The gal is so like me, yet so different. She's not too much younger than I am, although she is much better looking—almost regal. (On my best days, I'm more small-town-cheerleader pretty.) We're both in a line of work dominated by men. And we both talk tough.

The difference there is that my toughness goes about as deep as the makeup I wear. In fact, it's almost that exactly. Something I apply and wear throughout the day in order to fool folks. Deep down I'm about as soft as a cotton-swaddled baby's butt. I can't stand up for myself when it counts. And I can't say no to people, even to those who aren't any good for me.

But Gaia is truly tough. It's like the girl was poured into a cast-iron mold. She's confident and direct, and she can fight back, sometimes literally, when she has to. Plus I'm sure it takes a special person to handle FBI work.

I've seen many recruits in my days at the bar. In the beginning, those kids are all so young and green, so eager to prove themselves. But as the days tick by, they become more and more jumpy and bedraggled. That fussy, job-interview care with their appearance slowly gives way to a schlubby, just-showered-and-grabbed-the-least-dirty-pants-I-could-find-on-the-floor type of look. Dark circles appear beneath their eyes as if branded there—like some official FBI identifying mark. And then some of them, the most spooked-looking ones, stop showing up at all (and I know it isn't because they finished their training and got a cushy position at a faraway field office).

Only Gaia never showed any of those telltale signs. (Well . . . except for the dark circles.) She never seemed overwhelmed at all. If anything, her appearance improved. And her gaze grew steadier.

I have a feeling that Gaia could teach me a lot. I truly like her, and I know she's worth getting to know as a friend, but I also want to divine her secrets and see if that pluck could somehow rub off on me.

Besides, I can tell she needs a pal right now. Toughness aside, there's also a sad quality about her. Like a tiger that paces back and forth in its cage at the zoo. I always felt sorry for that poor cat, and now Gaia reminds me of that tiger.

And I'm thinking, maybe we can help each other. That or we can just have ourselves a grand time over some of my home-made mint juleps.

Sometimes just being together with a friend is enough.

"Wow. This is great, Kim."

Gaia was sitting cross-legged on her bed, reading over his latest report on the Lollipop Case. On her legs she balanced the bound stack of profiles printed from the disk. The sunshine poured through the tiny window in her dorm. It was a new day, and it felt good to be back on the case.

"You think so?" Kim eyed her warily. He'd been afraid of what Gaia might think about the work they'd done since she left. Even though she would have never come right out and accused him of doing subpar investigative work, he probably could have picked up her true feelings just by watching her. But right now, she truly seemed impressed. Almost . . . relieved.

"Yeah," she said, nodding. "Especially the dating service link. This is just the breakthrough we need."

Kim smiled. "I thought so, too." He'd been thrilled to discover that all the victims had been clients of the service. To him, it was one of those key puzzle pieces that revealed a huge section of the overall picture. But Will and his supersized ego never gave him the credit he thought he deserved. Either Will didn't have complete faith in Kim's investigative abilities, or he simply couldn't share the power.

Will. Just picturing his square-jawed, handsome face made Kim's insides writhe. He couldn't stop thinking about their confrontation the day before. It hurt that Will would accuse him of being underhanded—especially after everything he'd done for him. But then, maybe things wouldn't be this awkward forever. If Kim had gotten kicked off a high-profile case, he probably would have brooded for several days before accepting it. Maybe this was how Will had to deal. Maybe after stomping around and sadistically taunting people for a week or two, his ego would gradually inflate back to normal.

Maybe.

"So . . . I ran into Will in the weight room yesterday," he said, trying to sound matter-of-fact.

"Oh?" Gaia pretended to still be reading, but he noticed her eyes stopped moving. Her posture hardened almost imperceptibly.

"Yeah," he went on, staring at a tack hole above Catherine's bed. What had been there? "He . . . uh . . . wasn't all that glad to see me."

"Huh." Again Gaia seemed to toughen before his eyes. She glanced up at him, her expression blank and guarded. "What did he say?"

Kim rolled onto his back, folding his arms to cushion his head. "He was trying to cover his hurt feeling and make like he was teasing, but it was obvious he was pissed about being taken off the case. I know it's just a pride thing and I shouldn't take it personally. But I hope he can get over it soon." He turned sideways and saw Gaia staring out the window. Her expression had jetted several miles away. "So how are things between you two?"

"We're fine," she replied, scratching the side of her mouth. "Same as always."

Uh-huh. Her reply was a little too quick and packed with too much emphasis to be true. And people tended to unconsciously touch their faces when they were lying, as if trying to physically assist the words out.

Kim had been wondering if she and Will had taken their friendship to the next level. Now his suspicions were confirmed.

But why wouldn't she just admit it? Did she, like Will, also not fully trust him?

"Come on. How could you really be the same?" He sat upright again, instinctively running his hand over his hair to make sure he didn't flatten any of his moussed spikes. "Especially after everything you went through."

Gaia frowned. "What do you mean?" She seemed almost mad—the flimsy, reactionary kind of anger people used to cover up a hurt.

"I meant . . . you know. Staring down danger side by side? That's got to bring two people closer together."

Gaia's face seemed to crack from all angles. For a few seconds it looked like she might burst open, letting loose a stream of emotion. Then she blinked a couple of times and it was gone. "We connected," she said in an indifferent tone. "Nothing big."

"And now? Any weirdness about the Lollipop Case?"

Again Kim noticed a definite physical reaction. Her back bowed and her shoulders curved inward, as if his question had rammed her in the gut. "I haven't really seen him since we got back," she said with a lazy shrug. "We're both so busy, and I'm focused on getting this case solved before someone else dies."

"Yeah." He nodded as if he understood completely. As much as her evasiveness hurt, he knew better than to press it with her.

Get over it, he told himself. *So she doesn't want to open up about her relationship with Will. That doesn't mean she doesn't trust me.*

Or does it?

They were friends, after all—or so he'd thought. And now

they were partners. And Kim, with his gift for analyzing behavior patterns, could give her some real insight into her social life.

Of course, she could be doubting this ability of his. With good reason, too. He'd bonded with Catherine better than with anyone else on the base, and he'd never picked up on any duplicity. Some expert he was.

"Hey, Kim." Gaia suddenly bounced off her bed and headed to her desk. "Would you mind looking at something for me while I finish getting up to speed on the case?"

"Sure. What do you need?"

"I worked on my field report most of last night," she went on, flipping through some papers. "I think it's coming along, but now that I've read yours, I realize mine could be better. Do you think you could look it over and tell me where it needs work?"

"Sure." He could tell she was purposefully changing the subject, but no big deal.

Kim slid his legs over the side of the mattress and pushed himself upright. Gaia slid a stapled document out from under a stack of folders. She stared at it almost wrathfully for a few seconds before finally handing it over.

"Remember, it's just a first draft," she said. "I haven't had a chance to fix the grammar or anything."

He reached for the paper and almost had to tug it from her grasp. "I'm sure it's fine," he said, giving her a reassuring smile.

Kim slouched back against the wall and starting reading. At first he concentrated mainly on the grammar and mechanics, but he only added a comma after a lengthy opening phrase—and even that was simply to feel useful; he wasn't entirely sure it was needed. After a while he forgot the *way* it was written and got caught up

73

in *what* was written. The meeting with Marsh . . . the skirmish with agents on her tail . . . meeting up with Will and getting trapped inside the courthouse. It was amazing—like an extended episode of *Alias*. By the time he reached the part where the explosives revealed the underground bunker, Kim was perched at the end of the mattress, bent over the report as if it were a scandal-laden gossip rag.

He had known his friends weren in a dangerous situation, but he'd had no idea just how dangerous. They'd been completely outnumbered, with guns to their heads. Even though Gaia was an almost superhuman fighter (and Will, to a slightly lesser degree), it was unbelievable they could overcome such odds.

A strange, unsettling feeling was seeping over him like warm tar. Something he'd just read sounded strange. Kim returned to the top of the page he was on and reread the last three paragraphs.

"Um, Gaia?" His voice sounded strangely hollow. "Listen to this: '*While I distracted Marsh and Catherine, Agent Taylor managed to free his left hand from his bindings. . . . As one of Marsh's men bent over him, Agent Taylor incapacitated him with a quick strike to his larynx. He then commandeered the man's weapon.*'"

"Uh . . . sorry. Should I have said 'when' instead of 'while'?"

"It's not the grammar. It's the fact that Will actually disabled an armed guard with his left hand!"

"So? What was he supposed to have done? His other hand was still tied."

"But that's amazing. I took some judo and karate as a kid. Performing a precision move like that is incredibly difficult, especially if you aren't left-handed. It would be tough to get up enough power."

She gave a lackluster shrug. "I don't think he can, normally. It was probably just a surge of adrenaline. It happens, you know. The body can do some wild things when under extreme pressure."

Kim nodded. What she was saying made perfect sense. But still . . . His instincts were still sputtering over something.

He shook his head and ran his hand over his bristly hairdo. "I guess I'm a little freaked out about everything you guys went through."

Gaia's expression fell. "Yeah. Everyone's a little freaked, I think. Me, Will, Malloy, Bishop. First we go AWOL. Then we discover the whole Catherine-as-terrorist thing. There's a lot of freaking, but not a lot of trust." She gazed down at her hands distractedly.

Kim felt a pang of sympathy. He couldn't imagine what sort of emotional repercussions she was dealing with. "I trust *you*," he said, meeting her gaze.

For a second Gaia seemed almost sad. Then slowly her mouth bowed into a soft smile.

"I trust you too," she said.

Kim returned a wobbly grin. Was it his imagination, or had she hesitated a bit too long before answering?

George Clooney.

That's who Dr. Lehman looked like: George Clooney at age thirty.

For the past four minutes Gaia had been sitting across from the bureau staff psychiatrist, wondering who the hell he reminded her of. He had the same swarthiness. The same dark bedroom eyes, broad shoulders, and sultry features.

The only thing missing was that trademark scoundrel quality of Clooney's. Dr. Lehman didn't have the impish grin or smug stare. Instead he gazed back at her with perfect placidness. She could divine absolutely zilch from his smooth, serene expression. It made her wonder if he actually practiced his professional poker face in front of a mirror for hours and hours. Even his body language revealed no secrets. He sat utterly relaxed and open in his maroon leather swivel chair. Thankfully he did blink regularly; otherwise Gaia would have felt compelled to take his pulse.

"What were you thinking about?" he asked, tilting his head ever so slightly to the left. His voice was deep but had a boyish quality to it. It conveyed warmth, curiosity—even innocence.

"Nothing," she replied. She realized she sounded like a child, but she didn't want to tell him the truth—that she'd been wondering why the FBI would hire such a good-looking psychiatrist. It seemed almost a liability.

"Do you have any questions before we begin?" he asked, leaning forward slightly and meeting her gaze head-on.

"No," she replied, averting her eyes. She had to do well here without giving away any potentially damaging information. Her future at the FBI was on the line.

She looked past him and noticed a metal nameplate resting atop his modest wooden desk. *Greg Tyler Lehman* was etched on it. Greg, huh? She would have guessed a more lilting, soap-opera-type name. Like Seth or Blake or Remington. "Greg," with its single syllable and spit-producing consonants, sounded more appropriate for a football player. He even had the broad shoulders of a footballer, and his beefy chest was a little too snug in his powder blue button-down.

Not that she was staring. His pectorals just happened to be in her line of sight.

"Are you comfortable?" Dr. Lehman asked, dipping his head a little to meet her gaze. "You keep glancing around. Does being here make you nervous?"

Concentrate, Gaia. "I don't get nervous," she said with a frown, mad at herself for getting sidetracked. "You should know that." She was surprised someone as seemingly professional as this guy hadn't bothered to do any homework on her.

"Yes, I've read all about your unusual emotional nature in your file," he said, gesturing toward his desk without glancing at it. "But I didn't mean nervous as in fearful. I meant nervous as in uncomfortable—sensing a lack of power in a certain situation. I take it you don't like feeling powerless; is that a fair assessment?"

"It's fair," she said, meeting his gaze. "But I don't think powerless is how I feel right now. I would classify it more as . . . apathetic. I'm not a big believer in this sort of stuff."

She wasn't purposefully trying to be combative, just honest. Yet she was aware she was probably coming across as a smart-ass. She scanned Dr. Lehman for some subconscious sign of ire—a stiffening of his posture or a shift in his seating position. Instead a smile swept across his face. A completely warm and open grin.

"Fair enough," he said with a rumbly chuckle. "Then why don't we get started? You need anything before we begin? Water? A different chair?"

"No, sir."

"You don't need to call me 'sir.' Or even 'Dr. Lehman' or 'Doctor.' I want you to call me Greg. Okay?"

"Fine," she said.

"And may I call you Gaia?"

"You may."

"Well, then, Gaia." Dr. Lehman leaned back in his chair, signaling the official start of the session. "Why don't you tell me why you left Quantico four days ago without leave?"

Gaia felt a bit of a letdown. The question was so obvious and insipid; she'd expected better from him. "You know why. To save Catherine."

His eyebrows flew up. "To *save* her?"

"Yes. The FBI had written off the case as a kidnapping/homicide and wasn't looking into it any further. I had a gut feeling there was more to it than that, but I didn't have time to convince the bureau chiefs they were wrong. So I took it on myself."

"Why did you feel there wasn't time? What was the hurry?"

"Because they could have killed her at any moment."

"Who's 'they'?"

Another lame question. "The people who took her. Socorro."

"But nobody took her, did they? Catherine is a member of Socorro, isn't she?"

Gaia hesitated. Now he was getting to the hard stuff. He'd been setting her up with his easy questions. "Yes . . . she was. But I didn't know that at the time."

"Socorro staged it to look like she was kidnapped and then killed. Why is that, do you suppose?"

"So the FBI wouldn't go after her." *Duh!*

"Yet you did. They also planted enough clues to make you think she was still alive and in need of rescuing. Why did they do that?"

"To fool us."

"To fool . . . who?"

"Me! To fool me, okay?"

"How does that make you feel?"

"Just peachy."

He continued to sit and stare at her, completely calm and composed, awaiting a serious answer. Gaia was at first prepared to let him wait, but his expressionless gaze was like a hot beacon shining down on her. His droopy, oh-so-understanding brown eyes seemed to penetrate her defenses. Obviously she wasn't going to be able to get away with vague non-answers with this guy. She was going to have to clam up completely or lie to him.

Or . . .

There was a third option. She could, for the first time in her life, really give counseling a chance and open up—tell him the whole undistorted truth, no matter how unnatural that might feel. After all, she'd tried it last night with Kelly to a lesser degree and it had worked out fine. Great, in fact. And she'd confessed her fearlessness to Will a couple of days earlier. Granted, it had been to more mixed results, but the fact remained that for the very first time in her life she felt strong enough, trusting enough, to reveal her innermost secrets.

Maybe this was just what she needed in order to progress as a normal, healthy human. Some real emotional disclosure. Maybe if she continued to unburden herself to people, professionals especially, she could learn how to better navigate the strange and sometimes horrific twists in her life.

"Okay. I felt . . . used," she said finally.

"I see." Dr. Lehman's thick brows scrolled together over his nose. "And how did Socorro know how to use you?"

Gaia glanced down at her hands, still bruised from her fight in the courthouse. Her nails looked ragged and her cuticles were dry and split. More than any other part of her body, her hands belied her rough nature. She should really try to take better care of them.

"Gaia?" Dr. Lehman leaned forward, his face faintly creased with concern. "Did you hear my question? I asked why Socorro was so certain you'd take the bait."

"I don't know!" she snapped. She was telling the whole, plain, unpackaged truth. She really didn't understand how she could have fallen into their trap so neatly. But confessing it aloud dredged up all the shame and frustration she'd so successfully buried. It pissed her off that Dr. George Clooney was making her face it.

This was going to be more painful than she'd bargained for.

Dr. Lehman didn't seem the least bit fazed by her anger. "Maybe you would know why . . . if you let yourself," he said.

"I doubt it." Again Gaia scowled down at her hands. That was the thing. She was never very good at self-analysis. That was why she usually lied and manipulated her way out of these little talk sessions.

She was good at many things. Ask her to fight a pack of knife-wielding thugs? No problem. Challenge her to do a page of highly advanced calculus? Done. Demand that she keep her mental wits about her while getting sucked into quicksand? Piece of proverbial cake. But ask her to look inward? Insist that she study herself? That was when the GAME OVER sign flashed in big neon letters.

"As you know, the bureau asks all of its field agents to write a detailed analysis of their missions not only to document what happened for the official records but also for their own benefit. Sometimes when you write about something you experienced, it helps you understand it. Maybe you'll get some insight when you compose your report."

"Maybe."

"The answers are inside you, Gaia. Just listen to yourself. When I asked you earlier why you went AWOL, you said, 'To save Catherine.' I find it interesting that you use the word *save*. Do you feel it's your job to save people?"

"Isn't it? I mean, I am an almost fully trained government agent, after all."

"Yes, you are a rookie agent. But you didn't work within government protocol, did you? In fact, your file is full of instances where you took on a threat alone—as a vigilante, a lone ranger. Why didn't you work *with* the FBI to track down Catherine?"

"I told you already. Because it would have slowed me down. I thought her life was in danger."

"Yes, but the bureau could have also helped you discover the true intentions of Socorro. They might have also uncovered their plot to trap you. Right?"

"Possibly." Gaia felt itchy and squirmy all of a sudden. For the third time Gaia pondered her hands, staring hard at a little speck of dirt in the corner of her left thumbnail.

She heard Dr. Lehman lean forward in his chair. "Think, Gaia. Really think. Why was it so important for you to risk everything for Catherine, based on little more than a hunch?"

"I don't know." Gaia shook her head. Cooperating with therapists was actually more difficult than manipulating them.

"Just give me your gut reaction. The first answer that comes to you is typically the most honest."

She took a deep breath and launched the first word out of her. "Loyalty."

"That's very important to you?" he asked while scribbling something on his notebook.

"Yes."

He met her gaze again. "Then let's talk about loyalty. Who are you loyal to?"

She sighed impatiently. "The bureau. My country."

"You don't need to assume I'm looking for answers like that. You're doing well, Gaia. Just tell me the truth. Who are you loyal to, and why is it so important?"

Gaia remembered her heart-to-heart with Kelly the previous night. "My friends. They're very important. I guess because I don't make friends easily. So when I do, I just want to look out for them and protect them."

"From what?"

"Everything. From all the dangers that tend to follow me around. People in my past got hurt and killed just because they were close to me. I don't want that to happen anymore." She slouched over and rubbed her temples, suddenly weary.

"I see." Dr. Lehman nodded again—an academic type of nod, as if the motion itself helped him process the information he was being given. "So you look after them. But . . . who looks after you?"

Gaia's head suddenly snapped up, as if triggered by an invisible switch. "That's irrelevant. I don't need to be taken care of."

"You don't?" His eyebrows rose into distinct semicircles. "But doesn't everyone at some point? Why not you?"

"Because—" she began, then broke off, glaring fiercely at Dr. Lehman. For some reason, she was angry with him.

Dr. Lehman waited a few beats and then tilted toward her. "Because . . . ?" he prompted. "Because why?"

Gaia could only glower back at him. *Because of what I am!* she shouted inwardly. *Because I'm fearless!*

It was her penance for being different. Because she'd been born with this freak genetic anomaly, she didn't get to have things that other people deserved. Like a mother or doting father or normal, turmoil-free childhood. She wasn't sure who pronounced this sentence on her or when it had happened, only that it was there. Because she didn't feel fear, she wasn't allowed to ask for help.

Her eyes were suddenly brimming with tears, and something hard bottled up her throat. She didn't want to do this anymore. She'd followed orders and given therapy a real chance, but now she had an overwhelming urge to flee from the room.

Gaia was just filling her lungs to announce her departure when Dr. Lehman rose to his feet.

"Well, that's enough for today," he said, smiling down at her. "We can continue this some other time."

Gaia stood slowly, feeling a little shaken. In a way, she was disappointed the session was over—despite the fact that it had gone from awkward to excruciating. Something had happened here, only she wasn't sure what.

"You know, Gaia . . ." Dr. Lehman clasped his hands together and pressed them, prayer-like, against his lips—a textbook look of concern. "You don't need anyone to figure you out. But you really should listen to yourself more, get to know your own needs."

"Right." *Whatever that meant.*

"In the meantime here's my card." He pressed a rectangular piece of card stock into her battered hand. Gaia caught a whiff of his musky cologne. "It has my cell and home numbers. If you should ever have a problem but you don't want to go to your friends, you can always call me. I'll do whatever I can to help. And you won't have to feel protective of me. Deal?"

"Okay," she mumbled, stuffing the card into the front pocket of her shirt as she trudged toward the door.

Dr. Lehman crossed the room ahead of her. "Goodbye, Gaia," he said, holding the door open for her. "Take care of yourself."

"Goodbye, Dr. Lehman."

"Greg," he said, smiling broadly as she passed. "Call me Greg."

Session Notes
Dr. Greg Lehman
Subject: Agent Gaia Moore
Session Time: 0800 hours

Gaia is a challenging case study because of her unique emotional state. Because she does not feel fear, her stress manifests itself in extremely different ways. For one, Gaia appears to carry an overabundance of guilt. Today she admitted to having difficulty opening up to and bonding with others. Once she does make friends, she is intensely protective of them—perhaps because she has so few. In addition, this heightened need to preserve such relationships makes her quite blind to any faults or ulterior motives her friends might have.

Social boundary issues are another challenge Gaia has faced in her life. It appears she continues to grapple with them. Because most laws and limits are made in an effort to combat collective fears and create a secure-seeming environment, it is understandable that she either consciously or unconsciously does not feel they apply to her. However, it is my strong opinion that she is in no way sociopathic or in danger of becoming so. Instead the dangers of her circumventing protocol are hers and hers alone.

I hope to obtain Gaia's trust. Perhaps then I can help her better understand her own nature—all its blessings and burdens—and allow her to shrug off some of the weight she shoulders.

"She's allowed to watch *Blue's Clues* at nine thirty if she wants, but don't let her beg for more." Kelly leaned to the right and rebalanced her daughter, Jasmine, who was clinging to her left side like a baby monkey. "She'll probably be ready for an *n-a-p* in about two hours. And there some are sippy cups with apple juice in them in the fridge."

What on earth is a sippy cup? Gaia wondered. She stood grasping the arms of a dining room chair while Kelly trotted back and forth across the kitchen, finding her car keys and tossing dirty breakfast dishes into sink. It amazed Gaia that Kelly could do everything one-handed and with a tiny person on her hip.

If Gaia could have, she probably would have been scared. After all, she had never babysat anyone before. Of course, Kelly didn't know that. She assumed, like everyone else on the planet would have, that a woman Gaia's age would at some point in her life have cared for a child—if only for one evening.

But Gaia hadn't. Maybe it was because she'd never exuded a warm, nurturing nature. She had been one of those "troubled" teens: insolent, contemptuous of authority, and with a strong loner instinct. Mothers most likely saw her as a five-foot ten noxious contagion and feared any close contact would cause their children to become just like her.

So why did Kelly want her to babysit? She seemed like a smart gal. And she knew Gaia well enough to sense she had problems. So why was she entrusting her with the most valuable thing in her life?

Whatever the reason, Gaia told herself, *I won't let her down.*

"I promise I'll be back before dinner. Since my appointment is so early, the doc probably won't be all that behind schedule," Kelly went on, wetting a tiny cloth and wiping something that looked like grape jelly off Jasmine's cheeks. "You're so sweet to do this. Especially since you must have real work to do. *Important* work."

"It's all right. Today's a light day," Gaia lied. On the list of all possible jobs in the universe, catching a serial killer was probably right at the top. Gaia was unsettled by the reality that the Lollipop Killer could be casing his next innocent victim while she familiarized herself with sippy cups and the latest offerings from Nickelodeon. Still, Kim could handle things for a couple of hours, and they had plans to reconvene over the new evidence that evening.

The truth was, she really *wanted* to do this for Kelly. And this work was important, too.

"Jasmine, sweetie?" Kelly pushed wispy blond bangs out of her daughter's face. "Do you remember Mama's friend Gaia?"

The tiny girl shook her head rapidly, refusing to even glance in Gaia's direction.

Gaia figured she should say something—anything to break the ice. "So . . . how old are you, Jasmine?" she asked, stooping slightly to try and look her in the eye.

The little girl lowered her eyebrows sullenly and placed her head against her mom's shoulder.

Kelly jostled her daughter encouragingly. "Tell her, Jasmine. Tell her, 'I'm almost four.'"

Jasmine frowned at her mother. Her perfect forehead puckered into several folds and her lower lip jutted way out, overhanging her tiny chin like a poufy pink awning. It was such a dramatic display of ire that Gaia almost laughed out loud.

"And you thought I was sassy," Kelly said to Gaia. She shook her head as if exasperated, but Gaia could see the smile beneath her features. "Normally she's such a little chatterbox, just like her mommy. But she's mad at me right now for leaving. I don't get many evenings off to be with her, so mornings are supposed to be our special time."

"We're supposed to play Chutes and Ladders and eat Popsicles!" Jasmine huffed. Again Gaia stifled a grin. The little girl had the exact same cadence and eastern Virginia drawl as her mother, only higher. It was like hearing Kelly on helium.

"I know, baby. I'm sorry. Mama has to see the doctor sometimes just like you. Just to make sure I'm all right."

Gaia took a step forward. "Could I play Chutes and Ladders with you?"

Jasmine fixed her round baby blue eyes on Gaia, searching her face for a long moment. After a while her brow smoothed and her pouty lower lip relaxed into its proper place. She nodded at Gaia, slowly at first and then with increasing speed. "Okay," she said.

Kelly shot Gaia a look of surprise. "My, my. Normally she doesn't warm up to people so fast. You've definitely got the magic touch."

She set Jasmine down on her feet and kissed her forehead. "Okay, now. Mama's got to go. Here's some extra sugar for while I'm gone." She bent down and kissed her daughter's cheeks, brow, and mouth, then finished off with a nose-rubbing "Eskimo" kiss. "Rosy, rosy nosy!" the two of them said together, Jasmine erupting into giggles.

At least Jasmine seemed cheered up now. Gaia was beginning to think she could do this after all—as long as she didn't have to say things like "rosy nosy." Maybe somewhere deep inside her she did have some maternal instinct. After all, she did have the world's greatest mother for at least the first half of her life. It had to have rubbed off at least a little.

"Bye, baby!" Kelly called as she backed out the screen door.

"Bye, Mama!"

As soon as Kelly disappeared from sight, Gaia turned toward Jasmine. "So where are your games?"

"Over here. Come on." Jasmine grasped Gaia's hand and tugged her through the living room toward a set of warped, particleboard shelves. The top two tiers were stuffed with various Kelly items like a *Pretty Woman* DVD, a phone book, paperbacks with titles like *The Love Enchantress* and *Sighs of Solitude*, a few accordion files, and a squat, lopsided clay pot that could have only been made by Jasmine's little hands. The bottom two shelves were packed with picture books, puzzles, and games. Jasmine squatted down in front of the second-to-bottom shelf and expertly slid Chutes and Ladders out of a teetering stack.

"I want to be the little girl," she announced as she lifted off the lid. "You can be the little boy."

"Sounds good to me," Gaia said.

Fifteen minutes later Jasmine was already well on her way to winning. On her fourth turn she had landed on a square that illustrated a boy helping a kitten out of a tree. Because of her "good deed" Jasmine was allowed to climb a ladder that shot her fifty-six spaces ahead. Gaia, on the other hand, was moving forward one or two squares at a time.

"Uh-oh. You broke dishes," Jasmine said gleefully. "You slide down."

"Shoot," Gaia said, pretending to sulk.

It was starting to come back to her. Little snatches of memories—making cookies with her mom, trying on her mom's pearl necklace, studying her mom's face as she washed dishes while humming the aria from *La Traviata*. There was something inherently sweet about those shared moments, and Gaia could remember the snug warmth that would spread through her little body.

Now, with Jasmine, she hit on a small revelation: that perhaps those moments might have evoked similar feelings inside her mother. Even though Jasmine wasn't her child and she wasn't even close to being her parent, it still surprised her how much she was enjoying herself. It was a pure joy—uncomplicated and utterly rewarding. So very refreshing after the convoluted stresses of the past few weeks.

"Do you play this with your little girl?" Jasmine asked as she flicked the spinner with her index finger.

"No. I don't have a little girl," Gaia replied. "I don't have any kids."

"Do you live with your mommy?"

"No."

"Oh. Do you live with your daddy?"

"No. I live alone."

"Oh." Jasmine stared at Gaia so sadly that Gaia actually felt a small pang of self-pity. She realized the word *alone* was probably a scary word for an almost four-year-old. And as much as she valued her space, Gaia had to admit she was having a hard time adjusting to the aloneness of her life right now. She missed Catherine, even though she knew her former roommate's friendship had been mostly an act. And she missed Will, who was still clearly avoiding her. After spending all that time with him, she felt a little disconnected without him around anymore. Gaia kept telling herself he just needed some time to think straight—just like she did whenever she was upset. But she also couldn't help wondering if he might never come back to her.

Jasmine's reaction had been correct. Alone wasn't exactly scary, but it was strange.

"Did your mama and daddy go away?" Jasmine asked as she bounced her game piece three spaces ahead.

Gaia felt another tiny *ping* inside her chest. There was something about Jasmine's innocent questions and angelic voice that pierced right through to Gaia's heart. "No. Not exactly. My mom died a long time ago, and my daddy just lives somewhere else."

Jasmine nodded slowly. "My daddy does, too. But he used to live here." She looked up at Gaia and smiled. "Want to see?"

"Uh . . . sure."

Jasmine jumped up and trotted to the far side of the living room, her bare feet making light clapping sounds against the floor. Gaia watched as the little girl stood on her tiptoes and pulled open a heavy drawer on a side table. When she returned, she was holding a large, fabric-covered photo booklet.

"Look," Jasmine said in a hushed, almost reverent voice as she set the book on the floor and opened it up. "See here?" She pointed to the first photograph.

It was a photo of Kelly's wedding. She looked breathtakingly beautiful in a long flowing gown and flower garland. And she looked happy, too. Her face looked less careworn, and her smile was wider than Gaia had ever seen it.

"That's Daddy," Jasmine said, pointing to the man beside

Kelly. "Terrell Michael Mitchum. I used to be Jasmine Mitchum, but now I'm Jasmine Ray. Mama and I match now."

Gaia studied the man in the photo. He was skinny, with a long mullet and sideburns and beady, rodent-like eyes. His expression was one of strained acquiescence—a striking contrast to Kelly's eager joy. Even in a frozen, two-dimensional state the guy seemed like a major loser. Of course, she was probably predisposed to hate him. Gaia couldn't forget the way brittle lines appeared on Kelly's face whenever she talked about him.

"This is me when I was just a baby." Jasmine flipped forward five or six pages until she came to another photo spread. On the left was a department store portrait of Jasmine at about eighteen months. Her blond hair was in tiny piglets and a wide, open-mouthed grin pushed up her chubby cheeks. On the right-hand page were four candid snapshots. Three were of Jasmine and Kelly (who looked thinner and more haggard than in the wedding portrait), and one was of Jasmine and her daddy. He was sitting on the porch swing with Jasmine on his lap. But while the little girl wore a wide, cheerful smile, Terrell Michael Mitchum looked stiff and surly. Gaia could almost re-create the moment mentally. Terrell had probably been slurping Budweisers on the porch when Kelly came out with the baby and plopped her on his lap to take a photo.

She glanced over at Jasmine, who was also studying the picture. Her face looked somewhat wistful but not sad. Gaia felt honored that Jasmine trusted her enough to share this with her. She got the feeling that Jasmine sometimes needed to talk about her daddy but that Kelly wasn't too keen on the topic.

"Tell me about your father," Gaia said. "What is he like?"

Jasmine's eyes swiveled upward as she thought. "Loud," she said simply.

Gaia nodded. Her memories of her mother were extremely sensory, too. Whenever someone asked about her, Gaia would try to frame the description in grown-up terms, often relying on care-worn phrases like "full of life" or "a beautiful spirit." All true but way too vague to do her mother justice. When she really closed her eyes and thought about her, she remembered the sound of her singing as she cooked. So to Gaia, *loud* was a very good description of someone.

Gaia felt yet another tug inside her. She hadn't felt this tender toward someone since the day she found her long-lost brother. Jasmine was such an angelic creature, all rosy cheeks and clear, innocent eyes and pure spirit. She deserved a much better father. But then, so did many others.

Parenthood. What a job. I see people doing it all the time, but I rarely sit and think about what they're actually doing. I mean, sure, I've noticed the *motions* of parenting. The feeding and cleaning and comforting and scolding. But what I've never really thought about before is the emotional gamut of it all.

I joined the FBI because I admired people who gave unselfishly of themselves in order to improve the world. To me it seemed the ultimate duty. But I was wrong. Bringing children into the world and doing right by them is the ultimate duty. You risk so much more of yourself.

I read once that being a parent means going around with your heart outside your body. At the time I thought it a rather icky, melodramatic metaphor, but now I think I sort of understand what that means. It's a fear thing. Parents have to guide these precious little beings safely to adulthood, worrying the whole time about kidnappers, accidents, terrorist strikes, and subliminal messages in rock music. I always figured parenthood was hard—but I never realized how *terrifying* it must be.

That makes me wonder. . . . If I can't feel fear, would that handicap me as a parent? Sure, I could work out logically the threats my child faced—I'm not a moron—but without that paralyzing rush of anxiety it would all be academic. And what if all that worry is what truly makes people committed parents? After all, anything you're willing to risk pain for is automatically more valuable. Would that mean I couldn't effectively bond with my child?

I can feel everything else. I'm not a robot, either. I can feel love and joy and anger and sadness, so I would have other emotions at stake. But what if it's not enough? What if my freak biology makes me unable to develop key instincts?

Yet for the first time, I realize I might actually possess such instincts in a crude way. Playing with Jasmine feels so good. So natural. So easy. So *right*. I'd give anything to have such sweet moments on a daily basis. It made me realize . . . I would maybe, sort of, someday want my own child.

Not too long ago this subject wouldn't have even been a blip on my own personal radar. I never fully believed I would actually survive to adulthood, let alone create another life. Plus the concept of parenting typically involves having a partner. So even after I accepted the fact that I would have a future, I still saw it as a solitary one.

But now I've come out of my self-imposed loner existence and actually formed a relationship. And today my mind is beginning to stray into new territories. Namely ones involving picket fences and Volvo station wagons and a litter of small humans. It's all completely hypothetical, but it does bring up some pretty vital issues. Such as, *should* someone like me become a parent?

I have a lousy track record with relationships. If they don't leave me first, I almost always leave them—mainly for their own good. But it seems to me that once you have a child, there's no turning back. You can't break up with them, and you shouldn't push them away. Motherhood is one of those things you shouldn't do half-assed. You have to throw everything into it, really give up your innermost self. And let's face it, even though I'm great with physical risk, I'm crap at laying my emotions on the table.

So if I could be afraid, that is exactly what I would fear. Because the one main thing I learned from my own upbringing is this: parents go away. And if I ever failed my child—if my son or daughter ended up being the mess that is me—I don't think I could ever forgive myself.

There should be a rule. Ruin a kid's life, fall down a deep, dark chute. And never, ever get back up again.

ALL THE TRICKS

"Afternoon, Dr. Lehman."

"Please. Call me Greg," the guy said, holding out his hand.

Right. The standard we're-all-equals-here opening. How nice, Will thought as they shared a firm, football-player-type handshake.

Will hated this with a passion. It reminded him too much of his childhood. He'd been relatively fine until puberty hit and hormones turned him into a monster spaz. The change had happened almost overnight. Suddenly at age twelve he couldn't sit still in class, yelled out inappropriate things to get attention, and even once stole a fish. (It just seemed like the thing to do at the time.) His mother considered putting him on one of those designer drugs for hyper kids but eventually decided he just needed to "talk."

Thus began the years of counseling with various well-meaning but completely inept professionals. He'd quickly learned that if he simply clammed up, they would start postulating things on their own in an effort to validate their presence. Soon they'd have him all "figured out" when the only thing he'd said was "hi."

Of course, eventually he had gotten better—but it wasn't because of the counseling sessions. It was because he'd discovered the thrill of competing—especially in track. It forced him to dig down inside himself and kept him focused.

The guy sat back down in his chair and clasped his hands across his middle. "Do you have any questions before we begin?" he asked, opening his hands palms upward. *To show he has nothing to hide,* Will noted. *Classic body language to set me at ease.*

"No." Will glanced around the small office. Its warm green

walls, antique standing lamps, and wooden blinds were very soothing, while the floor-to-ceiling bookshelves and framed diplomas elicited a desire to improve oneself. And he liked the fact that the desk was pushed up against the wall instead of blocking the space between them. This guy was better than most.

"So how have you been doing, Will? May I call you Will?"

"Sure. And I'm fine," Will said, settling into his own seat.

"Great. Glad to hear it."

Yeah. I bet.

Will felt like a sullen twelve-year-old again. The only difference was that his feet now hit the floor while he was sitting down.

"Are you comfortable, Will?" the good doc asked. "Need anything before we begin?"

"Nah. I'm fine," Will replied.

He'd be an obedient pup and play along, just long enough to get his clearance for field duty. He would only divulge the tiniest bit of information—just enough so the doctor would feel like he'd actually done something. He should say he'd been having trouble sleeping. Yeah. That should do it. Then Dr. Feelgood would say some words of encouragement about how time would fix everything and hand him a prescription for a week's worth of Xanax. Mission accomplished.

"Why don't you tell me about what happened in Pennsylvania?" Greg said, leaning way back in his chair as if he'd just popped open a bottle of Budweiser and wanted to discuss the Redskins.

Will shrugged. "What's there to tell?" he replied, trying to match Dr. Lehman's easygoing pitch and cadence. "I'm sure you've read the report."

Dr. Lehman seemed unperturbed. "I'm aware of the facts, but

I don't know anything about your real experience. Tell me. Knowing everything you had to risk, why did you go rogue and meet up with Gaia?"

At the sound of Gaia's name Will instinctively ducked his head and stared down at the multicolored rug thrown on top of the dull industrial carpeting. He wondered how Gaia's session went with Dr. Lehman in the morning. Had she told him everything? No. Somehow he knew she hadn't.

"Will? Are you going to answer?"

There was no trace of impatience in Dr. Lehman's voice, but still Will felt annoyed.

"I don't know."

"You don't know if you're going to answer or you don't know why you went rogue?"

Will had to stop himself from smiling. Yep, he was definitely twelve again, hoping to get a rise out of some nosy adult. "Just . . . I don't know."

Dr. Lehman nodded thoughtfully, as if it was the most interesting answer he'd ever heard. "I see." He rested his right elbow on his armrest and propped his chin in his right hand. "Tell me about your relationship with Gaia. How would you describe it?"

"I don't know," Will said again. This time it was the truth. He was still trying to be evasive, but he honestly had no idea where things stood between him and Gaia. He wondered if Greg already knew they'd slept together. Surely Gaia hadn't told him. But he might have guessed. Or someone might have been tailing them to make sure they did return to Quantico after going AWOL.

Maybe that was why Malloy and Bishop busted up their partnership. But if so, why didn't they say that?

After Malloy took him off the case, Will couldn't help but feel lessened—in Gaia's eyes, his superiors', and his own. He was robbed of the chance to shine, to solve the case and be the hero. He didn't blame Gaia, but he still felt sore at her for some reason. He didn't want to be with her, yet he missed her. It made no sense. Nothing made sense right now.

"I imagine everything must be pretty confusing after all that you've gone through," Dr. Lehman continued. "Would you say that's a fair assessment?"

Ah. Now he was soliciting his approval. The old we're-in-this-together style of treatment. This guy knew all the tricks.

Once again Will didn't respond. Forget it. Let the professional hypothesizing begin. Let 'Call Me Greg' do all the talking while he zoned out.

"I wonder, is your stress job-related or something more . . . personal?"

Will forced himself not to look at Dr. Lehman. It really did seem like he knew everything.

"That's one of the biggest problems in our line of work," Dr. Lehman continued. "Not blurring the line between our work and our social lives. And that's one of the reasons why we offer these sessions. So you can work out the stress of dangerous field missions here and not burden friends and family with it."

A small snort escaped Will's nostrils. "What do you know about dangerous field missions?" he asked. He realized he was breaking his silence, but he couldn't help himself. He had to put this guy in his place.

But Dr. Lehman just smiled. "It may surprise you that I was a field agent for four years before finishing my psychiatric studies.

I understand quite well the immense mental stress caused by dangerous missions. That's why I came back to do this. I want to help agents deal with all that."

"Good for you," Will said, not even trying to hide his snide tone. It almost seemed like Dr. Lehman had set him up for that little revelation. Not only did he get Will to speak, he also managed to divulge his do-gooder calling. What'd the guy expect, anyway? A medal? Applause?

Dr. Lehman didn't even flinch. "I remember putting my friends through hell back in the day. I just got so used to keeping my guard up to protect myself in the field. But when I got back home, I didn't know how to let it down again."

Will pondered the tiny green light flashing on the sleek laptop on the desk. He was attempting to appear uninterested, but he found himself listening closely in spite of himself. He didn't know how to shake loose his stress either. It wasn't just the danger he'd been in or getting taken off the case—it was everything. He had no sense of himself anymore. He felt like that computer screen—dark and empty, with only the smallest ember of life beating inside him.

"Eventually I learned how to separate things out," Dr. Lehman continued, leaning back in his chair. "I realized it wasn't fair to take the pressures of the job out on friends and family since they really had no part in it and inversely, that it wasn't fair to bring my personal problems into work with me. It was hard, but after a while I could make that transition. It's like turning off a light as you leave a room and turning on another as you enter a new room."

Funny he would mention lights. Will was still mesmerized by the pulsating green glow on the Dell. *Go on,* it seemed to be telling him. Will turned toward Dr. Lehman and opened his mouth, ready to voice the question that had sprung up in his mind. But words failed him.

"Go ahead, Will," Dr. Lehman encouraged in his Quaalude-smooth voice.

"Okay, fine," Will began. It wasn't like he was actually going to let the guy analyze him. His question was more . . . hypothetical. He took a breath and plunged. "What you're saying sounds all fine and dandy, this whole separating business and personal life, but what if you end up having problems with someone who's both a work partner and a . . . friend?"

Dr. Lehman eased his chair forward and smiled. "You have to figure out if the problem is a business one or a personal one. Then you proceed from there."

Session Notes
Dr. Greg Lehman
Subject: Agent Will Taylor
Session Time: 1400 hours

Like most recruits, Will is a person of considerable ego who does not appear to have had much experience with failure. At present, the principal source of his anxiety seems to be Agent Gaia Moore. It is not clear what their relationship is, but it appears to go beyond that of partners. Will undoubtedly has strong feelings for Agent Moore, although it's not certain whether Agent Moore shares the same feelings.

Obviously Will is grappling with the stress of the mission and its aftermath, but he seems to be fixated instead on the tensions between him and Agent Moore. This could be an evasive maneuver on his part, an attempt to avoid processing deeper anxieties. Or it could be that he is easily handling the mission but having difficulty with more personal troubles.

It is unclear whether Will is aware of Gaia's unusual genetic makeup. Either way, my concern is that he is enchanted by her fearlessness and that his competitiveness will impel him to take unnecessary risks. Therefore, I support the decision to prevent these recruits from working together on future missions.

"Where's Jasmine?" Gaia glanced around the living room, pretending not to notice the wiggly bulge beneath the afghan throw. "Jasmine? Oh, Jasmine?"

The bulge giggled.

At least she's getting better, Gaia thought. Jasmine's previous hiding place had been behind the see-through shower curtain in the bathroom.

"Hmmm. Is Jasmine under the table?" Gaia asked as she stooped to look beneath the round oak dining table. "No," she added as if bitterly disappointed.

The blanket laughed and thrashed.

"Oh, I know!" Gaia exclaimed. "Jasmine must be in here!" She opened up the pantry door and peered into its dusty depths. "Aw, no," she went on. "Not here either."

Another muffled squeal came from beneath the afghan.

Gaia continued to pace the hardwood floor of the kitchen-dining area. "Could Jasmine be . . . in the trash can?" She quickly lifted the plastic lid off the waste can and peered down at the pile of wrappers and coffee grounds.

"No!" said a distant, giggly voice. "That would be yuck!"

"Well, I give up," Gaia mumbled dejectedly. "I guess I'll never find her."

"Here I am!" Jasmine exclaimed, throwing the blanket off her.

"Oh my!" Gaia jumped back and pressed her hands to her chest. "You surprised me! I'm so glad to see you!"

Jasmine rocked back and forth, laughing her beautiful

glockenspiel laugh. Her wispy golden hair stuck out at odd angles, making her look like an oversized dandelion.

Just then a knock sounded on the back door.

"Mama!" Jasmine started trotting toward it.

"Wait, no." Gaia reached out and grabbed her shoulders gently. "It's too early to be your mama. And your mama has a key, remember?"

"Oh, yeah." She looked from the door to Gaia, her eyes growing wide and round. "Who's banging?"

"I don't know, but let me check. It's sort of my job."

"Okay."

Gaia walked over to the back door and pulled back the checked curtain on the window. "No way," she mumbled. Standing on the porch with his thumbs hooked in the belt loops of his faded Diesel jeans was Will.

He smiled weakly when he saw her and lifted his right hand in a wave.

A light, warm squeezing sensation came over her—like a ghost pain from when he'd held her close only two nights before. She was sincerely glad to see him, but she was also still smarting from his cold-shoulder treatment. Strange. She'd been waiting for this reunion for two days, only now that it was happening, she wasn't sure what to do. Kiss him? Punch him? Both?

She unbolted the door and opened it wide enough to poke her head out. "What are you doing here?"

"I came to see you." His shoulders hunched slightly, and he shifted his weight from one worn running shoe to the other. "I was thinking maybe we could . . . talk?"

Gaia stared at the crack of skin visible at the top of his shirt where two buttons were undone, and a warm tingle oozed over her. *Talk?* The word echoed in her mind as she wrenched her eyes back up to his. Yes, talk would be good. It was what normal people did in order to maintain their normal relationships. She was better at punching, and she'd rather just kiss him, but a meaningful conversation was probably the best way to go.

"Okay," Gaia replied, opening the door.

Will stepped into the house and glanced around. "Where's Kelly?"

"She had a doctor's appointment."

Jasmine skipped into the room and cocked her head at Will. "Who are you?"

"Well, hello, there, darlin'." Will crouched down and smiled at Jasmine. "I'm Will. I'm a friend of Gaia's. You must be Jasmine."

"Uh-huh." She nodded rapidly. "I'm almost four."

"Almost four? Wow. Are you having fun with Gaia?"

"Yeah! She was looking for me in the trash can!"

Will shot Gaia a baffled look.

"Long story," Gaia told him. She and Will exchanged smiles, and another rush of heat swept over her. She was pleased to feel their previous connectedness returning. A talk should nudge everything back into place. If only they could grab a little privacy. "Hey, Jasmine," she said, stooping over and tousling the little girl's blond hair. "Your mom said you could have a Popsicle later on, and now it's later on. Want one?"

"Yeah! I want orange! I want orange!"

Gaia opened the freezer and pulled out a long, bullet-shaped orange Popsicle. "Let's go out on the porch and eat it, okay?" she said as she unwrapped it and handed it to Jasmine.

"Okay! Okay!" Jasmine said, jumping up and down and reaching for the Popsicle.

The three of them stepped out onto the long wooden porch that hugged the front of the house. Gaia handed the Popsicle to Jasmine, who immediately went skipping into the yard with it. Meanwhile, Gaia and Will sat down on a creaky, warped pair of rocking chairs.

For a while they just sat there and rocked and watched Jasmine pick up a few of her scattered toys and sit down beneath a skimpy oak sapling. While she waited for Will to say something, Gaia savored the languid pace of the moment. They could be parents watching their child at play. Or grandparents rocking away the afternoon. It was a whole different speed than she was used to at Quantico. And now that Will was here, most of the gloom and confusion that had been weighing her down the past couple of days was rising off her with every dip of the rocker. She was a hair's breadth away from total joy—only her innate cynicism prevented her from completely giving in to the moment. That and the fact that Will hadn't actually made his intentions clear yet.

She was pretty sure Will had come to make things right between them. He hadn't apologized, at least not yet—and knowing Will's ego, he might not ever. But he had a definite sheepish air about him.

"Cute kid," Will remarked, nodding toward Jasmine.

"Yeah." Gaia grinned as she watched the child. So carefree. So innocent. All FBI recruits should be required to do this occasionally. It was good for the soul. "So how'd you know where I was?"

"Kim told me."

"He told you I was here?"

"Well, not exactly. He said you were helping out a friend. The rest I figured out on my own using my brilliant, well-honed investigative skills."

"What a genius. Must have been tough remembering that Kelly's the only real friend I have besides you and Kim." She turned and peered at Will's profile. "How was it with Kim anyway?"

He flashed her a hangdog expression. "You heard about us squaring off in the gym that day, huh? Yeah, well, he's still kind of chilly toward me. Not that I blame him. I wanted to lash out at someone that day, and he was just in the wrong place at the wrong time."

"I get it."

They rocked in silence some more.

"So what did you want to talk about?" Gaia asked, not wanting the silence to stretch on too long.

He grimaced slightly and shifted in his chair. "I wanted to tell you . . . I'm sorry. I've been a real horse's ass since we got back to Quantico."

"Is this the part where I'm supposed to argue with you and tell you that you weren't that bad?"

"I suppose, but you get a pass this time." He rubbed his palm over his flat-top haircut and stared down at his lap. "I was just . . . I don't know . . . embarrassed, I guess. I know you had nothing to do with my getting kicked off the case, and it was unfair of me to blame you. Sometimes it's just hard for me to get past my competitive nature. But the thing I finally realized is"—he lifted his gaze to hers—"I don't want to *compete* with you. I want to *be* with you."

108

Gaia stared into his bright blue eyes for several beats before cracking a huge smile. "How long did it take you to rehearse that?"

Will grinned impishly. "Only a couple of hours," he said, shrugging. "But I mean it. I've missed you these last couple of days. And the missing-you part was stronger than the humiliation-and-envy part."

Gaia blew out her breath and stared up at the cloudless blue sky. Utter happiness was again reaching out for her, but her negative polarity was still in the way. "But can we do this?" she asked. "Can we be a couple? For real?"

"Hell, why not? That's the one good thing about not being on the case together. We don't have to worry about being un-professional."

He's right, Gaia thought. *There's no reason why we can't make this work.* Her final shroud of doubt was lifted, and relief and joy spread through her limbs.

She stared out at Jasmine, who was sitting on the grass, eating her Popsicle and playing with a naked Barbie doll. The heat had made the Popsicle melt faster than she could eat it, and her face and hands were an orange, sticky mess. Several blades of dead grass had stuck to her cheeks, making her look like a bearded garden gnome.

It's the simple things in life that matter, Gaia thought as she watched the little girl. *Things haven't exactly been simple with Will. But maybe they can be now.*

"Gaia! Push me on the swing! Push me! Please?" Jasmine leaped to her feet and raced over to a tire swing hanging from the broad lower limb of a nearby maple.

"Aw, let me," Will said. "Gaia doesn't know how."

109

He loped over to Jasmine, lifted her into the swing, and slowly pulled it as far back as it would go.

"Be careful," Gaia called. "Don't hurt her."

"She'll be okay. Jasmine's an expert swinger, aren't you, Jasmine?"

"Yeah!"

"All right. Hold on tight now. Ready, set . . . go!"

Will let go of the swing and Jasmine sailed far forward, her fluffy blond hair waving in the breeze. Jasmine let out a high-pitched squeal—a mixture of surprise and all-out glee—and kicked her tiny feet up and down as she cruised. "Again! Again!" she cried. "Do it again!"

Gaia laughed as she watched them from the porch. Will was really good at this. It was amazing how at ease he was around kids.

She had to admit, she found this new side of him quite attractive. It made him seem so much more affectionate and carefree. And far less self-centered than he usually came across.

Once again Gaia felt like she was living in a parallel universe. One where she and her husband were out playing with their small daughter on a beautiful sunny morning.

Only this time, it didn't seem so implausible.

he's here somewhere

"I can't believe how many people use this dating service," Gaia mumbled.

She and Kim were sitting at a table in the mess hall, poring over page after page of profiles from the Second Chance dating service. Kim had managed with Lyle's help to extract the names of all the clients who had either dated or researched the murder victims. The resulting list came out to over one hundred names, which they had color-printed and divided up between them.

"Don't get too caught up in this," Kim advised. "Just separate out anyone who seems the least bit suspicious. We have to narrow this down some way."

Gaia nodded. She knew he was right. Spending the day playing pretend family with Will and Jasmine must have made her extra contemplative, and she was having a tough time getting into that detached frame of mind their work required. Instead of thinking of these profiles as possible suspects, she saw them all as people—lonely people who were willing to do anything to find a special connection with someone else. That or she was turning into one of those annoying people who wanted to see everyone happily matched up just because she was in a good relationship. Either way, she couldn't help but feel a little sorry for them.

Of course, one of them very likely didn't deserve her pity. One of them was quite possibly preying on other lonely types. Killing single moms who were not only struggling to find their own happiness but struggling to create happy lives for their children, too.

She had to focus.

"Here's a guy who was a left-handed pitcher in high school," she said, holding up the page for Kim to see. "What do you think?"

"That's enough. Put him in the pile."

Gaia set the page atop Jerry Heinz, the wrestler; Marcus Lowery; the history buff who made swords in his spare time; and a whole slew of avid fishermen.

She turned to the next profile and began reading:

Roger Conroy—age 38—artist—loves long nature walks, reading poetry, and playing Frisbee.

She stared at the accompanying photo. Roger was definitely going for the country rebel look that was all the rage around here, complete with battered Stetson and a shirt that looked like it had been cut and sewn from a Texas flag. And he was definitely *not* thirty-eight. He was forty-four at the very least. Perhaps he thought he could suck in his gut and avoid direct sunlight long enough to fool someone. Gaia couldn't understand why he didn't just tell the truth, but she supposed he had his reasons. And he wasn't the only one who fictionalized himself.

She sighed and placed Roger facedown on the "no" pile. Looking at the photos was making her a little sad. Some opted not to submit any at all. Of those who did, several sent in pictures that were soft focus or clearly dated. A few were candid shots, but most were posed. The men had fresh haircuts, a gleam on their cheeks from a recent shave, and a look of cloaked despair verging on panic behind their eyes.

But so far none of them looked like killers.

"So how did babysitting go?" Kim asked, keeping his eyes on the profile before him. "You didn't have to change any diapers, did you?" A tiny smile was curving his lips.

"Pull-ups."

"What?"

"Jasmine's done with diapers," Gaia explained. "She wears these things called pull-ups. They're, like, transitional diapers. Learner's permit underwear."

"Oh. Did you have to change those?"

"Thankfully, no. She did get kind of messy eating a Popsicle, though. But Will got her cleaned up before Kelly came back."

Kim's head snapped up. "Will showed up? He came looking for you, but I wouldn't say where you were. I figured you would have told him if you wanted him to know."

"It's all right. He figured it out himself." She smiled at him—an action that was a whole lot easier now that she and Will had made up. "Don't worry. Everything is fine between us. It was weird for a while, but he apologized. Sorry I didn't tell you before. I was still sorting it out myself, you know?"

"Yeah," Kim said. "Glad to hear it's all good now." His mouth stretched into a tight smile. She could tell he was trying to look happy for her and failing miserably.

"He also said he felt bad about the way he treated you," she added.

"Really?" Kim's eyebrows lifted in surprise and then fell, meeting in a grim line above his nose. "He didn't say that to me."

"I'm sure he meant to," Gaia said, noting how defensive she sounded. "He probably will soon—in his own way."

Kim nodded sullenly as he refocused on his reading, effectively ending the conversation.

Gaia looked down at the papers in front of her. She glanced over the profile of Dennis Ambrose, age thirty-five (more like forty), senior management assistant (desk jockey), who looked like Ronald McDonald without the makeup. A frown pulled down her features as she read his personal interests statement. "Listen to this, Kim," she said. "This guy says, 'I'm looking for a real woman who knows her place. I want kids, and I want a woman who will stay home and raise them. I expect to be the sole breadwinner and head of the household just like the Bible mandates.'" She looked at Kim's thoughtful expression. "What do you think? Sound psycho-killer to you?"

"Not exactly. Misogynistic? Yes. I don't think our guy would be that up front about his contempt for women. He isn't careless or showy in the way he kills. But put that guy in the pile anyway." He sighed and dunked a soggy Tater Tot into the small pond of ketchup on his plate. "I know he's here somewhere. I just wish we knew how to set him apart from the rest."

"I know what you mean."

Gaia set Dennis Ambrose in the stack of other possible suspects and turned to the next profile.

Mike Mitchell, age thirty-two. As she glanced at the photo to see if he looked his stated age, a cold tingle swept over her. She'd seen the guy before. Thin build. Pinched features. Rat-like eyes.

"Oh my God. It's *him*," she said in a loud whisper.

Kim set down his papers and looked at her quizzically.

"Who?" He craned his head, trying to see what she held in her hands.

"It's Kelly's ex-husband! His real name is Terrell Michael Mitchum."

"Are you sure?"

"Yes! Jasmine was just showing me photos of him." She squinted down at his frozen, smirking expression. Just looking at his ferret-like face dredged up a deep, almost animal-like hatred. Only two hours before she'd been playing with this man's child. She'd been helping out his ex-wife—a wonderful woman whom he had sorely mistreated.

Gaia's limbs buzzed with the familiar buildup of adrenaline. It was as if her own body was sounding an alarm, warning her of something dire and preparing her for a fight.

"Kim," she half whispered, her voice weak from the seismic activity inside her. "I think we found him."

His forehead creased with doubt. "That's not enough, Gaia, and you know it. You can't just go on a feeling. I know Kelly is a good friend, but—"

"It's more than that!" Gaia glanced around and then leaned forward across the table, lowering her voice. "We know he's hiding something since he isn't using his real name. Plus he checked 'single' instead of 'divorced,' and he lists himself as having zero kids. And Kelly is always talking about what a creep he is."

Kim nodded. "Okay, he's definitely shady. But serial murder? What motive would he have? It's not that I don't believe you; it's just that we've got to go by the book. We're on thin ice with the bureau and can't afford any mistakes."

Gaia's fist tightened on her napkin. Kim's calm, reasonable

arguments were frustrating the hell out of her. "Okay, then," she said, talking a deep breath to curb her restlessness. "As far as motive, couldn't he be getting back at Kelly in some twisted way? Kelly said he threatened her a lot during the divorce."

"Then why doesn't he go after Kelly?" Kim asked. "Why go after all those other women?"

"I don't know! You're the profiler!" Gaia's high-octane adrenaline was suffocating the last of her patience. Right now she wanted to act, not talk. Terrell was bad news, that much was clear, and her gut was telling her he was up to something. And her gut was never wrong. Hardly ever. "Look, it's not *impossible* that he's seeking revenge, right?"

Kim gave her a conciliatory nod. "Okay, well, sometimes there are cases of *displaced* rage where the killers target *substitutes* for the real object of their wrath." He took the profile from her hands and studied it intently.

"Come on. It's worth checking him out, isn't it?" Gaia asked, practically bouncing in her seat.

Kim let out a long, weary sigh. "Okay. Let's go talk to him."

Yes! Gaia leaped up from her chair.

"But." He held out a hand, stopping her. "Promise me you'll behave yourself, okay?"

"Don't worry," Gaia replied. "You can count on me."

FACES DEVOID OF EMOTION

"Slow down, Gaia!" Kim yelled as Gaia took a turn at sixty miles an hour. Luckily his shoulder strap engaged, preventing him from slamming against the passenger side door.

"What?" Gaia asked, frowning. "I'm not even speeding."

"Technically you are. You're supposed to decelerate for turns."

"Whatever."

This was a bad idea, Kim told himself as he straightened his suit jacket. He glanced over at Gaia and studied her profile as she drove.

He'd known Gaia long enough to recognize that look—that fired-up Valkyrie-riding-into-battle look. All she needed was a metal-plated bra and a white steed instead of the bureau's Chrysler sedan loaner.

Of course, Gaia's constant need to keep moving was one of the things he liked about her. When spurred to action, she was a force of nature, right up there with F5-category tornadoes and giant tsunamis. He, on the other hand, was more cerebral—maybe too much so. Before doing anything, Kim liked to consider every possible outcome in his mind. He was more prone to reacting too late, whereas Gaia usually ran the risk of reacting too soon. Maybe that was why they were made partners. They balanced each other out. The FBI's version of the Odd Couple.

"I think this is it," Gaia said, her voice practically sizzling with anticipation.

They drove past a homemade wooden sign that read, White Pine Park, Next Left. Half a minute later they came upon another homemade sign, this one just a hand-painted orange arrow pointing down a dirt road. Gaia swerved around the corner, causing Kim's shoulder strap to hug him tightly once again.

"Uh . . . you're going to be able to keep cool with this guy, right?" Kim asked as he continued to scrutinize her body language. Not only was Gaia battling the adrenaline of their first hot lead in a long time, but the heat of potential payback for Kelly lit a fire in her eyes.

"Of course," she said, frowning slightly but otherwise not moving at all. She was still hunched over the steering wheel like a jockey, her knuckles white from gripping the steering wheel so tightly.

"It's just that . . . you tend to get ultra-protective of Kelly. Remember that time you went all kung fu on her bartender?"

"That guy was way out of line. I just sort of . . . pushed him back in line."

"Fine. Whatever," Kim said, holding up his palms in a gesture of surrender. "All I'm saying is that even if you *intend* to be calm, it might be more difficult than you think."

"Don't worry. I'll be the consummate pro," she said, smiling at him. Kim could tell she was trying to look composed, but her grin looked somewhat manic. Her mouth was a little too tight and her eyes were a tad too focused.

Gaia drove into a gravel parking lot and parked the car between a ramshackle van and a 1970s station wagon with the wrong size tires mounted on it. In the time Kim took to unbuckle his seat belt, Gaia had already jumped out of the car and was stalking toward the "park," a weed-choked field crammed with trailers, Airstreams, and RVs of various sizes. The trailers were parked in two straight lines with a wide path in between.

"Which one is his?" Kim asked, jogging to catch up.

"Number nine," Gaia replied.

As they stepped off the gravel lot onto the grassy area, their shoes sank in the moist dirt. *Why did I wear my best Doc Martens?* Kim moaned inwardly.

He glanced at the squalor all around him—the sagging, dilapidated homes and muddy, trash-strewn yards—and instinctively focused on the weight of his Walther inside his jacket. He hated to admit it, but places like this gave him the creeps. He told himself that it was because of his well-honed perception, that he simply intuited people's despair and misery to an agonizing degree. But maybe he was a little prejudiced, too. His upbringing had been so sheltered, so upper-middle-class spoiled, that scenes like this only existed at a safe distance—in books or movies or the safe distance of a TV news reel. Perhaps after existing in a world where his greatest stress had been nailing a sonata in time for his next music lesson, it was only natural he should feel rattled by such surroundings.

As he and Gaia walked down the path between the rows of trailers, they passed an older couple sitting on lawn chairs in the shade of their mildew-stained Gulf Stream.

"Afternoon," Kim said, nodding at them.

Neither of them responded. They simply watched him and Gaia pass, their eyes dead staring and their faces devoid of emotion.

Next they passed a woman wearing curlers and a dress at least one size too small. She was smoking cigarettes while hanging clothes out to dry on a makeshift line strung from the roof of her trailer to a nearby barbed-wire fence. As she glanced up at them, Kim greeted her with a smile and nod. The woman frowned fiercely, her face disappearing behind a thick exhalation of smoke.

This was not one of those happy campgrounds full of

free-spirited, nomadic wanderers who liked seeing the world through the windshields of their Winnebagos. There were no flowerpots or freshly swept entrances, no children romping happily in the sunshine, no beauty. This was a human dumping ground. A place for people who had hit rock bottom and had nowhere else to go.

Kim felt simultaneously depressed and repulsed—then guilty for having such a reaction. If he wanted to be an agent, he really had to deal with this aversion of his. After all, lots of investigations would likely lead him to these kinds of places.

Or was that prejudiced of him to even think so?

"Here's number nine," Gaia said, stopping in front of a shabby trailer that had probably once been blue but had weathered down to a somber slate gray. She walked up the trailer's fold-down steps and rapped loudly on the metal screen door.

"Federal investigators. Please open up," Kim called out, his voice weaker and shriller than he meant for it to sound.

They were met with silence. Kim leaned sideways and tried to peer through the grime-streaked window, but it was too dark.

Gaia lifted her fist and knocked again. "Open up," she shouted.

This time they heard a distinctive thud from somewhere inside, followed by muffled cursing and an irregular rhythm of footsteps. "Damn it, Leon! Is that you?" came a croaky voice from the other side of the door.

"Federal investigators, sir," Kim shouted. "Would you please open up?"

There was a long pause. Kim could almost feel the man's panic through the building's prefab exterior. "Uh . . . just a moment," the voice cried out.

They could hear his footsteps again, doubling in tempo, as he moved back and forth inside the trailer.

"Sir, open the door now!" Gaia yelled. She stepped back and looked the door up and down as if calculating the force needed to bust it down.

"Gaia," Kim said in a low tone, grasping her by the arm.

Just then the door cracked open and a man stood before them. It was the same man in the photo Gaia had shown him earlier—Mike Mitchell, a.k.a. Terrell Michael Mitchum—only he looked like he had just been awakened from a deep sleep. He was shirt-less and shoeless, his eyes were bloodshot, and small tufts of his greasy hair stuck out at odd angles. He looked from Gaia to Kim and back again.

Gaia glared back at him, her chin slightly raised and her hands tightened into fists. Terrell didn't seem to know what to make of her. Kim could almost see his brain sputtering. *Gorgeous woman on my doorstep . . . giving me the evil eye . . . looks like she wants to hit me . . . but damn, she's hot!*

"Yes, sir, and, uh . . . ma'am," Terrell said, rubbing his hand over his stubbly chin. "What can I do for y'all?"

The man was clearly uneasy—terrified, even. Although he was managing to keep his voice steady, his panic revealed itself in his jerky movements, his darting eyes, and the nervous way he worked his jaw as if chewing something. Every one of Kim's instincts sent up warning flares.

Since it was apparent Gaia was already locked in "bad cop" mode, Kim decided to be the calm, affable one. "Sir, I'm Agent Lau, and this is my partner, Agent Moore," Kim said. "We're with the FBI." He held up his badge for the man to see.

More jumpy movements. Terrell scratched his head and shifted his weight on his bare feet. "The FBI? Well . . . my, my." He chuckled uncomfortably. "What's all this about?"

"Sir, we'd like to ask you a few questions about an investigation we're working on," Kim said. "May we come in?"

"Eh . . . sure!" Terrell opened the door and motioned behind him with an erratic flourish. "Make yourselves at home!"

Kim and Gaia walked past him into the dim interior of the trailer. Almost instantly Kim was overtaken by a strong stench, a mixture of mildewed carpet odor and something else—a sharp, fusty smell like that of sour milk.

The place was a dank, disgusting mess. The narrow living room seemed to be where all the junk food containers went to die. Dirty clothes were scattered about like debris from a shipwreck, and the grizzled brown carpet, where visible, was covered in multicolored granular detritus.

There was no place to sit. The only piece of furniture besides a relatively nice plasma screen television set was a long, sunken couch. The cushions were completely piled with something that Terrell had hidden beneath a stained, yellow blanket.

"Afraid I can't talk that long," Terrell said, standing in the path to the living room. "Gotta be somewhere in a few minutes." Kim was now close enough to smell the bourbon on his breath.

"We won't take long," Kim assured him. "We wanted to discuss your use of a dating service called—"

"What's that?" Gaia asked suddenly.

Both Kim and Terrell looked at her. She was pointing toward the couch.

"I . . . I don't know what you're talking about," Terrell said nervously. He sidled to the left, positioning himself between Gaia and the sofa.

Kim glanced in the direction she indicated but saw nothing but Terrell's mess.

Gaia ignored Terrell. She walked toward the sofa and bent down.

What the hell is she doing? Kim thought in a panic. They had no warrant. They had no business doing anything but questioning the potential suspect—and even then, it had to be with his cooperation. She should know that. "Uh . . . Agent Moore?" He stepped into the living room. "Perhaps we should—"

"Look!" Gaia leaped to her feet and thrust her hands out toward Kim. In her left hand she held a knit cap, and in her right hand she held a knit sweater. She glanced past him, glowering. "Damn it, Kim! Where'd he go?"

"What?" He spun around. Sure enough, the screen door was wide open and Terrell was nowhere to be seen.

In a swift, cat-like movement Gaia sprang past him and raced out the door. Kim followed.

He squinted into the sun and caught sight of Terrell racing down the alley between the rows of trailers. Gaia was several yards behind him but closing fast, and Kim was several yards behind her. They passed the grouchy lady hanging laundry and the old couple in their saggy, woven lawn chairs—who still barely blinked as they watched the chase.

As soon as he hit the gravel parking lot, Terrell slowed slightly, clearly hampered by his bare feet and winded from trying to run in his inebriated state. That was just the break Gaia needed. From his vantage point behind her, Kim watched as she put on a burst of speed. Once she got within a couple feet of Terrell, she launched herself forward and tackled him to the rocky ground.

"You!" he could hear her shout. "You squirrelly, greaseball mother—"

"Gaia!"

Kim finally caught up to them, and not a moment too soon. Gaia was in full-on vengeful goddess mode. She had Terrell pinned down against the gravel on his stomach and was yanking his head back by his hair. "You're going to pay for what you did to them!" Kim heard her yell.

Terrell was struggling as best as he could but mainly ended up face-first in the gravel. "Get off!" he shouted, flailing his arms and landing his elbow in Gaia's ribs. Gaia reeled back slightly from the blow, allowing Terrell room to twist his upper body around enough to throw a few wide punches.

Kim reached into his jacket and slid his Walther out of its holster, training it on Terrell. For some reason the gun felt heavier than it did during training sessions, and it wobbled slightly in his grasp. The run hadn't tired him, but his breathing became fast and ragged. It was his trusty weapon, and his movements were exactly the way he'd practiced them at Quantico, yet he couldn't shake loose the thought that he was holding in his hands the power to end someone's life.

Do I shoot him? Kim panicked. He knew he needed to help his partner, and he was well within regulations to fire on someone attacking an agent. But his aim was all over the place. What if, instead of incapacitating Terrell, he killed him? Or missed and hit Gaia?

Only he needn't have worried. After a couple of Terrell's weak blows landed on Gaia, Kim saw a change come over her. For a split second he thought he even saw a smile flit across her lips. Then it was like someone hit a giant fast-forward switch.

Gaia disappeared, replaced by a blur of color and whirling limbs. She hit him once, twice, three times, then somehow flipped him onto his stomach, bending his arms back behind him. Terrell screamed in pain and terror.

"Gaia!" Kim cried. "Stop! You can't hurt him!"

Gaia froze in mid-fight and blinked hard a few times. She staggered slowly backward.

"Gaia?" Kim watched her stumble slightly. Her expression slackened, and her gaze grew dim.

"Not now!" she grumbled, still blinking and shaking her head.

Something was wrong. Terrell noticed, too. Kim saw him slowly lift his torso, his eyes darting about, looking for a new escape route. What now? If Gaia was suddenly out of it, that meant Kim would have to do something. And he could barely keep his arms raised as it was.

He heard a faint crunching noise and saw Terrell grabbing handfuls of gravel. Just then, something seemed to click inside him. "Lie down, Mr. Mitchum!" he heard himself shout. "Let go of the rocks and put your hands behind you!"

Terrell hesitated, as if pondering how this new voice could have come out of Kim.

"I said *down*," Kim repeated. He set his foot on Terrell's back and placed his weight on it, thankful he could finally muster up some intimidation. Terrell cried out, more in surprise than in pain, and Kim quickly grasped his wrists and clamped the handcuffs on him.

"Good job," Gaia said in a wheezy voice. "You take it from here, okay?" She glared down at Terrell's sprawled form as she slowly backed away.

"What? Where are you going?" Kim asked.

She turned and began lurching up the gravel path toward the parking lot. "I'll be in the car," she called over her shoulder. "I just need some time to lie down."

"What's going on?" Terrell whimpered, his nose still pressed into the dirt. "What just happened?"

"Beats the hell out of me," Kim said as he hoisted Terrell onto his feet. He returned his gun to its holster, grabbed Terrell's arm, and began steering him toward the car, pausing to wave at the couple gaping from their lawn chairs.

up to no good

"You're going to *what*?" Gaia's voice echoed off the cinder-block-walled corridor of the Quantico sheriff's office. But she didn't care. All she wanted was for Sheriff Parker to take back what he'd just said—to laugh and slap his knee and tell her it was all just a bad joke.

Instead he frowned and his bushy eyebrows lowered behind his eyeglasses. "There's no reason to shout, Agent Moore. You know as well as I do that you need to have strong evidence to back such charges. And a ski cap and sweater are nowhere near sufficient. Hell, if they were, we could hold half the men in this town."

"But he had links to the women! And he took off! He ran!" She clenched her fists. Seeing Terrell had dredged up so much anger that her adrenaline had seemed to run out prematurely—before she had a chance to capture and cuff him.

"Gaia," came Kim's whispered warning. He stood beside her as if at attention with his back straight, feet firmly planted and apart, and arms clasped behind his back. Just being in the sheriff's presence seemed to bring out the teacher's pet side of him. But she didn't care about scoring gold stars. All she wanted was to make sure that evil weasel in the cell down the hall never got a chance to hurt someone again . . . especially Kelly and Jasmine.

The sheriff heaved a lengthy sigh—as if the past forty-five minutes of dealing with Gaia had sapped him of all his strength. "Agent Moore," he began, his voice low and tentative. "Isn't it entirely possible that he ran because he assumed you'd found the stash of car stereos and other stolen equipment he'd hidden beneath the blanket?"

Gaia pursed her lips. "Okay," she admitted. "So he was hiding stolen equipment. Isn't it still possible that he's a thief as well as a killer? Maybe he stole things for a living, but he killed for revenge."

"That may be the case, but we have nothing to tie him to the actual killings. Nothing except conjecture and a profile at a dating service."

"But . . ." Gaia's chest was heaving. A logical voice in her mind was warning her to stay calm, urging her to remain professional. But in searching Terrell's trailer, she had found a printout of Kelly's online profile. It was clear that Terrell was up to no good.

True, she didn't exactly have the necessary proof to link him to the Lollipop Murders. No weapon or telltale bloodstains or eyewitness report. But the minute she came face-to-face with Terrell Michael Mitchum and looked into his rodent features, she knew she'd found the killer. Why else would she have such a strong reaction?

"We understand, Sheriff Parker," Kim said in his honor-roll-student voice. Normally she admired his professionalism. But right now it made her want to squeeze his throat. "Don't we, Gaia?"

Gaia clenched her teeth to prevent herself from arguing further but managed a slight nod.

"We are grateful for you two bringing him in," Sheriff

Parker continued. "We have all the proof we need to hold him for theft, but we can't hold him too long. If and when he makes bail, he will be released. But in the meantime, if you should find any solid evidence—"

"We'll have it for you," Gaia interrupted. "We'll find whatever you need. Just promise me, please, that you'll call us if he makes bail?"

"Now, that I *can* do," he said, nodding.

"We really appreciate your assistance in this matter," Kim said, holding out his palm for a handshake.

The sheriff gave his arm a manly up-and-down pump. "Just doing our job." With a tip of his hat he turned and strutted back down the hall.

Kim let out his breath as if he'd been holding it in the entire time. "Jesus, Gaia. Did you have to jump down his throat like that? Do I need to remind you of the thinness of the ice we're standing on with Bishop and Malloy?"

Gaia's stared at the sheriff's retreating backside. "We're supposed to be solving the case, aren't we?"

"You know the sheriff's only doing his job, too. You've got to have the evidence or the charges won't stick. That's basic, Gaia. Investigative Work 101."

She turned to face him. "Then let's keep digging." She shouldered her leather briefcase and began stalking down the corridor toward the elevator. "We've got to go back over the contents of his trailer and talk to people who live around him."

"Hang on a sec." Kim jogged up beside her and glanced at his watch. "You're not talking about doing all that right now, are you? Because I'm starving."

"You go ahead and get something to eat and meet me back here." The elevator doors parted, and Gaia stepped inside the metal cubicle.

"But . . . where are you going?"

"To see an old friend," Gaia replied.

Gaia watched Kim's bewildered expression disappear as the doors slid shut.

Kim

My first week at Quantico, I actually made notes on everyone I met, psychoanalyzing them just for kicks. I don't do it anymore, mainly because I got too busy. But recently I went back and read those passages in my notebook to see how accurate I was.

This is what I wrote about Will:

It's was obvious after two minutes that Will Taylor is a golden boy looking to find new glory. Sure, he wants to help people, but he also seems to crave the hero worship that comes with it. He sees all aspects of training as a competition and has one of those insatiable egos that thrives on challenge and success.

I was right—although it was fascinating to watch him deal with Gaia stealing the spotlight now and then. I think it made him get over himself and mature quite a bit.

The first note I made about Gaia was this:

Gaia is the toughest girl I've ever met and the toughest to try and figure out.

I never could self-assuredly analyze Gaia. It was one of the few times I'd been stumped. I could see she was clearly here to succeed—but not for any personal glory or attention. She appeared duty-bound but for darker, more complex reasons. She was obviously on some sort of mission, but toward what? Or *from* what? I could never tell.

Here it is, weeks later, and I still can't crack her.

Like now, on the Lollipop Case, her fixation on Terrell Mitchum tells me she's overcompensating for something. I can't tell for sure, since she doesn't display the usual signs of a past trauma, but I would guess that she's trying to make up for some past wrong, consciously or not. And because of this she can't see how off base she is.

But then, who am I to doubt her hunches? Maybe my inability to understand Gaia has more to do with my shortcomings.

Because this is what I wrote about Catherine that first week:

Catherine Sanders is the kindest, most genuine, most well-brought-up recruit here. I have a feeling she and I will be close friends for a long time. . . .

I should have seen through it. If I had, this whole Socorro fiasco could have been prevented from the start. But I let myself be duped. Maybe I was just so homesick and in need of friendship that I refused to question her motives. Or maybe I'm just not as good at this as I think I am.

THIS ISN'T OVER

Gaia knew she probably should have told Kim that Catherine had been brought into Quantico late last night, but she hadn't. If she had, he might have wanted to tag along. But Gaia wanted her visit with Catherine to be just the two of them. An epilogue to their long, maddening showdown.

Catherine hadn't seen her yet. Gaia stood in the shadows watching her former roommate as she sat on the floor of the dusty cell. Her back was to the wall, and her left elbow was propped on her bunk. Her left knee was bent, but her heavily bandaged right leg stuck straight out in front of her like some stiff, inanimate thing—a broom handle or a closed umbrella. Gaia felt a sudden surge of sympathy, knowing Catherine would remain in a cell for the rest of her life.

Catherine looked pitiful. Her close-cropped hair stuck together in clumps all over her scalp, and her standard-issue orange prisoner jumpsuit hung loosely from her thin shoulders. But what really changed her appearance was the absence of her glasses, which lay on a steel table next to her cot. They had always been part of her image—the way they framed her eyes and added sharp angles to her otherwise round, babyish face—making her seem like the coolest of the smart girls or the smartest of the cool girls. Without them her face looked exceedingly innocent. Gaia could easily picture her as a child, skipping around after her father, eager to absorb his knowledge and carry out his twisted plans in a blind effort to please him.

Gaia knew what it was like to grow up with secrets and deceptions. Catherine was just another one of Marsh's victims. He'd hijacked her mind, deprived her of a real childhood, and molded her into an unquestioning servant. Of course she hadn't resisted. Every girl wanted to please her daddy—something Gaia understood firsthand. But maybe there was still hope.

"So how's the food?" Gaia asked, stepping out of the dark recess toward the cell.

Catherine's eyes squinted at Gaia's shape. She reached over, snatched her glasses off her bunk, and put them on. "Gaia," she said, her voice devoid of emotion. Immediately the little-girl quality was gone, replaced by Terrorist Catherine—the toughened soldier Gaia had met in Socorro's underground headquarters. "Come to gloat, roomie?"

"Why would I do that?" Gaia asked. She pulled up a nearby plastic-and-metal chair and sat down, resting her elbows on her knees.

Catherine shrugged. "Because you probably assume you won. After all, I'm locked in here. Ramon is still in custody. El Dia was thwarted—for the time being."

"I'm relieved your plan was foiled. But I don't like seeing you here."

"Yeah, right," Catherine said with a snort. "Then why'd you come? Wanted to relive old times?"

Gaia was taken aback by the acid in Catherine's voice. She'd hoped that somewhere in the cavernous depths of Catherine's psyche—beneath all the layers of conditioning—remained the kind, decent young woman she'd roomed with. The one who'd encouraged her, consoled her, put her ass on the line with her. And idiotic as it was, Gaia still felt ashamed for having misled her in the bunker. Catherine had seemed so happy about the thought

134

of Gaia joining them. She imagined Catherine's life must be a lonely one, and having a friend for a comrade would have lessened the gloom a bit. Gaia had not only foiled their plot, she'd dashed Catherine's hopes as well.

Gaia must have made a face because suddenly Catherine's mouth widened and her eyebrows flew up into perfect semicircles. "Why, Gaia. You're upset!"

It physically hurt Gaia to admit it, but it was true. She had never had much success with girlfriends. The closest had been Mary Moss, whom she'd seen die at the hands of a scuzzball that Gaia had spared once too often. There had been other girls who had somewhat befriended her, even come to her aid, but it was always for a limited time and with a whole knitting basket of strings attached.

She had really thought Catherine would be different. In Catherine she had thought she'd found a lifelong friend, a true confidant who would support her professionally and personally. She'd envisioned them continuing to room together beyond Quantico and engaging in such female bonding rituals as sharing boyfriend advice, loaning each other clothes, and doing whatever else real girlfriends did for each other. Kelly had reached out to Gaia in that way. And now it as Gaia's turn to repay the favor.

"You're angry because I deceived you, aren't you?" Catherine went on, her brown eyes flashing in the dim light. "But then, you know all about deception, don't you?"

"I did what I had to do to survive," Gaia said, leaning back in the chair and crossing her legs. "But what about you?"

Catherine smiled enigmatically. "It isn't over. My dad is still free, and that's all that matters."

Gaia rose to her feet and ventured a few steps closer. "Come on. He doesn't care about what happens to you. That was obvious when he left you behind on the street after Will shot you." She regretted her words as soon as they slipped past her lips. After everything that had happened, Gaia still couldn't enjoy hurting her former friend.

"He did the right thing!" Catherine hissed. "Dad knew he had to keep going. That I *wanted* him to!" Placing her hands on her bunk, she struggled up to a standing position and hobbled toward the front of the cell. "If you think you're somehow better than me just because I'm in this cell, you're wrong!"

Gaia frowned. "I don't think I'm better than you. I feel sorry for you."

Catherine's face twitched angrily, and her pale skin burned crimson. "Save your pity, Gaia!" she snapped. "I don't need it. I manipulated *you*. And you were so easy. I was almost disappointed. All I had to do was tell you about my search engine and then disappear mysteriously. I knew you'd go to the laptop eventually. I just buried the antiterrorist files along with my remote access trail and *voila*! Down the rabbit hole you went!"

She paused, studying Gaia as if searching for signs of distress. Gaia met her gaze steadily. Catherine wasn't hurting her—not really. She was only poking a wound that had already been made.

"I was always the better agent," Catherine went on. "Do you know how hard it was, holding back my abilities so you wouldn't get suspicious? I could have won every obstacle course race. I could have solved the Hogan's Alley case. I could have even solved the Lollipop Murders. But I had bigger things to focus on."

Fire suddenly erupted in Gaia's gut. "Are you saying you could have solved the Lollipop Case but didn't *want* to?" she asked, striding up to the cell.

"That's *exactly* what I'm saying." Catherine seemed to notice that she'd finally struck a nerve. She started laughing, a shrill, taunting laugh that seemed completely incongruent with her pretty, pixie-like face.

Again, just like during her meeting with the sheriff, a shaky, helpless anger flooded Gaia's systems. Her hands itched to reach through the bars, grab Catherine, and shake the information out of her. She realized that was exactly what Catherine wanted. To get a rise out of her.

Gaia let her hands fall down to her sides. "You're bluffing. You don't have crap."

A deeper red shade crept over Catherine's face and neck. "Oh, it's there," she said. "Right under your nose, in fact. But you're way too much of a newb to find it."

It? So it was a thing. But what? A piece of evidence? Right under her nose?

Gaia gripped the bars and pulled her face up to Catherine's. "You're better than this," she said in an urgent whisper. "I know you. You're a good person, Catherine. If you have any information that might help us nab this guy, you should tell me right now! Tell me before another innocent woman has to die!"

Catherine cocked an eyebrow at her. "Trust me. You don't know anything." She stretched dramatically. "I'm going to take a nap. And you, I'm sure, still have lots and lots of work to do." She hobbled over to the bunk and lay down. "Good night, Gaia. Try not to blame yourself too much when it's time to ID another body and console another new orphan. The fact is, you'll never be a good enough agent to solve this case."

Gaia felt her mouth fall agape as Catherine crawled underneath a gray wool blanket. She was suddenly sure of one thing. The friendship they once shared had never existed at all.

THE PRESSURE INSIDE

Gaia recognized the staccato knock on her door and threw it open.

"Hey, gorgeous. You ready to . . . uh . . ." Will paused and stared her up and down. "Is that what you're wearing?"

Gaia stared down at herself. Her navy slacks and matching blazer were a definite FBI agent costume, not date attire. "I just got back a minute ago and didn't have time to change. Sorry."

"Oh?" Will's eyebrows flew up. "Big day, huh? Any breakthroughs on the case?"

Gaia bit her lip. "I can't really talk about it. You know that." She sighed and added again, "Sorry."

He opened his mouth to protest but suddenly thought better of it. "Right. I understand." He nervously straightened his tie. "Okay, so you want some time to change?"

"Can't I just go wearing this? I'm starving." Gaia's arms fell to her sides. Her face was tired and creased.

Will put his arms around her and pulled her up close. "You can wear anything you want. In fact, we can make this evening clothes optional, if you like."

Gaia laughed in spite of her sadness. "That would definitely limit our choice of restaurants."

"Who needs restaurants?" Will murmured in her ear, sending warm vibrations through her. "We can stay here and raid the vending machines." He began kissing her neck, moving slowly downward.

Gaia closed her eyes, trying to lose herself in the sensations. But images of the day kept wheeling through her mind, like snapshots in a scrapbook. Jasmine . . . Kelly . . . Catherine . . . When her brain hit on Terrell's pasty face, her body instinctively went rigid.

Will pulled back. "Whoa. What'd I do?"

"Sorry." Gaia shook her head, trying to knock loose the memory of Terrell's sneering expression and rancid breath. "Just . . . bad day. I guess I'm a little tense."

He cupped her chin and grinned down at her. "It's okay. Come on. Let's get you out of this place."

Gaia let him lead her out of the room and down to the parking lot. She felt comforted by the weight of Will's arm around her shoulders and enjoyed the ease of having someone else take control. Still, thoughts about the case kept coming—dive-bombing her and preventing her from fully relaxing. She had an uneasy feeling she was forgetting something vital.

"Here you go," Will said as he walked her up to the passenger side of his truck and unlocked the door. He opened it up and gestured to the seat with an exaggerated flourish.

Gaia climbed inside, pushing aside several items to make room. Binders, empty plastic bottles of Gatorade, a laptop case . . .

Something pinged inside Gaia's brain, as if a tiny switch had been thrown. That was it!

By the time Will was climbing in on the driver's side, she had already pulled out her cell phone and was frantically punching in some numbers.

"So I was thinking we might—" Will paused as he caught sight of the phone in her hand.

Gaia put her hand over the mouthpiece and smiled apologetically. "Sorry. This will just take a sec."

Just then a voice came over the receiver. "Lab," someone said impatiently. Gaia could hear the familiar clacking noise of a keyboard in the background.

"Lyle? It's Gaia. Listen, we need to take another look at Catherine's laptop. I think she might have found something— something that will help us with the Lollipop Case."

"Uh . . . like what, exactly?"

"I'm not sure. Catherine said I would never find '*it*.' That made me think it's something you can see, like a piece of evidence. Knowing her, though, it's probably something technical, which is why we need to go over everything on her hard drive."

Will started the engine and backed the truck out of the parking space. He appeared to be concentrating on the road, but Gaia could tell from his posture that he was focused on her conversation.

"I hate to say it, Gaia, but I really don't think so," Lyle replied. "We've already gone over it pretty good."

"But this is Catherine. She practically lived out of that laptop. And she said I was too much of a 'newb' to solve the case—another reason why I think it's something computer related. The evidence is probably there, but it's encoded or encrypted or something. Is there a way you can check for that? I know that if anyone can find it, it's you."

"Well . . ." She heard a rush of static as he sighed into the receiver.

"Listen, I know I've put you in some tough positions, and

you've always come through for me big time. You have no idea how grateful I am for all your help."

"I'll try. But I seriously think you've been duped, Gaia."

It wouldn't be the first time. "Just give it a go. Please? I'll come by tomorrow afternoon to see what you've found."

"Okay. I just hope you aren't disappointed."

"Me too." She closed up her phone. For a second longer its power display glowed alien green, then dimmed completely, like a candle being snuffed out. Maybe Lyle was right. Maybe she was just grasping at straws. But she had to follow every single lead, no matter how weak it seemed. She had to keep Terrell behind bars.

"You talked to Catherine today?" Will asked, staring at her uncertainly.

"Yeah." She repocketed her phone and stared out at the twilight, trying to ignore the sense of urgency that was building inside her chest.

"Guess you can't elaborate, huh?"

"Not really."

"Fine. I get it. So . . . where do you want to go?" Will asked. A grin spread across his face, gleaming in the dusky light. "I was thinking we could try Lombardo's again, or there's this one Mexican joint that people say—"

"How about Johnny Ray's?" Gaia asked suddenly. She had an idea of how she could alleviate some of the pressure inside her.

"Uh . . . seriously?" Will's dimples faded. "I mean, that's fine and all. It's just that I was hoping for something . . . nicer. But hey, if you're in the mood for cheese fries—"

"It'll just be for a moment. I need to talk to Kelly about something, and then we can go wherever you like. Okay?"

"You mean . . . you need to do more work?" Will asked. It seemed to Gaia that the light suddenly drained out of him, just like her cell phone.

"Please? It's important."

He exhaled heavily. "Okay," he said.

For the rest of the drive he sat stiffly in his seat, concentrating on the road and making no further attempts at conversation. Gaia knew this wasn't the best way to start a romantic date, but Will had to understand. He'd been there. He'd worked on the case. He knew how important this was.

Didn't he?

A DARK FORCE

Johnny Ray's was packed by the time they arrived. The dinner regulars were there—potbellied locals in non-ironic trucker hats and flannel shirts, as well as the happy-hour crowd, which were mainly trendy, professional types, including some trainees Gaia recognized.

"I'll grab a beer and find a spot somewhere else. You just tell me when you're done."

His tone was understanding, but his eyes looked weary and defeated. As he turned away from Gaia, she reached out and grabbed his arm.

"Hey," she said, stepping sideways into his view. "Thanks."

His mouth curled into a semi-grin. "No problem," he said before loping away.

Gaia still wasn't convinced that he was okay with the situation.

She knew Will well enough to tell when he was bruised. He was putting on a grand show of good attitude for her benefit.

I'll make it up to you, Gaia sent silently. *Just hang on.*

She turned and searched the restaurant for Kelly, finally spotting her behind the bar. She was chatting with a couple of locals while refilling a couple of mugs of beer.

As Gaia approached, Kelly caught sight of her and grinned. "Hey!" she called out. "Good to see you! What can I get for you?"

"Nothing, actually," Gaia replied. She reached the bar and squeezed in between a couple of patrons. "But I do need to speak with you. In private."

"Right now?" Kelly's face dimmed, just as Will's had earlier. Gaia was beginning to feel like a dark force of nature whose mere presence could sap people of their inner radiance and joy.

"Please? I know you're really busy, but it won't take long. I promise."

"Okay," Kelly said, eyeing her warily. "There's no privacy out here, though. Come around the bar and we'll go in the back."

Gaia veered around the bar and followed her into the kitchen, blinking at the sudden brightness of the fluorescent lights and the hazy steam that filled the air.

"Walter, Jorge, go take a smoke break," Kelly said to two aproned men who were working the grill.

The two men stared at each other quizzically. "But it's the supper hour," one of them replied, a big burly guy whose forehead was pouring with sweat.

"I know. This will only take a minute. Go out back and have a cigarette now, both of you."

The men shrugged at each other. "Okay," said the big guy. "But I got a couple of burgers on. Can you watch them?"

"Can do." Kelly watched as the two men ambled out the back door. A gust of evening air breezed in, dispersing some of the steam and clearing the air. As soon as the door squeaked shut, she turned to Gaia. "Now, what's this about? This doesn't have anything to do with Jasmine, does it?"

"No." Gaia shook her head vigorously. "I mean, not exactly. I'm here on business."

Kelly's eyes widened. "Business? You mean, FBI business?"

Gaia nodded. "Listen. We arrested your ex-husband today, and I just wanted to ask you a few questions."

"Terrell?" Kelly's eyes grew even larger. "Where was this?"

"He was in a trailer park off Highway One."

"I had no idea he was that close." She turned and stared at a rack of spices, shaking her head slowly. "That slimy piece of work." She frowned and looked back at Gaia. "So what did he do?"

Gaia took a moment to gather up the right words in the right order. It couldn't be easy to hear that the former love of your life, the father of your child, was potentially a psychotic killer revenging his unrequited love. She instinctively reached out and placed her hand on Kelly's left shoulder. "Terrell was brought in for theft and . . . suspicion of homicide. There was some circumstantial evidence linking him to the Lollipop Murders."

"Murder?" Kelly said almost soundlessly. The gleam in her bright eyes seemed to fall into shadow, and again Gaia felt like the Grim Reaper.

She watched Kelly closely, prepared to hold her, comfort her, or catch her in a faint. To her surprise, Kelly shook her head vigorously. "No. I don't believe it."

Gaia frowned. "He also had a copy of your online dating profile inside his trailer. Has he reached out to you at all in the last few months?"

"No." Kelly let out a long, tortured sigh. "I'm not saying he was a saint, Gaia. But I know the man, maybe even better than he knows himself. He's a horrible husband and a lousy father, but he could never purposefully kill anyone." She marched over to the grill and began flipping a set of burgers. Loud sizzling and sputtering noises drowned out the last of her words.

"I know this is hard to hear, but I need you to stop and think for a moment," Gaia said as the sizzling sounds ebbed away. "Do you know anything that might be important in this case? Anything he might have said or done?"

Kelly pushed a few stray hairs off her face, now damp from the steam. She stared down at her hands and sighed. It seemed to Gaia that she looked suddenly weary. "He could get mean; that's true. He got lousy drunk and hit me one too many times. So I left."

"Didn't you say he threatened you, too?"

Kelly grimaced slightly as she looked Gaia in the eyes. "Sure, he did. But he was scared. I was leaving him and taking his baby away from him. It hit him suddenly that he'd screwed up big time and was going to be alone. But after all was said and done, I never heard from him again."

She hunched over the grill again and absently scooted the burgers around. Her features sagged as if pulled down by a weighty sadness.

"I'm sorry," Gaia said again. "I know this isn't fun. But considering what I found, I wanted to let you know that there's a chance Terrell might make bail in the near future."

Kelly looked confused. "Really? He might get out?"

"Yes. And if he does, promise me you'll stay far away from him. Okay?"

"Don't worry," Kelly said, her usual sass starting to stir again. "He knows better than to mess with us anymore."

"Good. I'm glad to hear it. But still, let me know if anything weird happens, okay?" Gaia held her gaze. "And if you remember anything that might help—anything at all—just call me."

"Jasmine's been asking about you," Kelly said, grinning. "Can I call you to come babysit again?"

Gaia smiled. "Please do."

While Kelly went outside to fetch her short-order cooks, Gaia went back into the restaurant to find Will. She found him at one end of the bar, slumped on a stool and looking rather forlorn.

Gaia forced a smile as she approached him. "All finished. Let's go eat."

He shook his head. "I just called Lombardo's, and they're booked for the rest of the night."

"I'm sorry." Gaia felt a plummeting sensation in her gut. It seemed all she'd been doing that night was apologize.

Will gave a feeble shrug. "Yeah, well . . ."

Gaia glanced around. "Maybe we can just stay here and split a burger platter?"

"Just like always." He sighed and stared down at the tabletop.

Again a swooping feeling came over her, as if she'd landed in one of the long chutes in Jasmine's board game. Will was pulling away again; she could feel it. By doing her best to build a case against Terrell, she'd effectively ruined her date with Will—a date that was supposed to repair the rift that had been made before.

"I'm sorry," she said again. "I know you, I mean *we*, wanted something more special, but I had to come here and . . . I had no idea it would make us . . . I'm just sorry." She sat down in the booth and put her head in her hands.

She owed so much to so many people. She owed everything to Malloy and Bishop for giving her another chance after all her colorful and somewhat legendary errors of judgment, she owed it to Kim to be a consummate professional instead of the half-crazed lioness she'd become, she owed it to Kelly and Jasmine to keep a close eye on Terrell, and she owed Will a date—a real date. But most of all she owed it to Ann, Laurel, and Terri to push past her own problems and nab their killer.

"Hey. It's all right," Will said while stroking her hair. Gaia glanced up and noticed he was smiling—not an all-out happy smile, but a small-yet-genuine one. He cupped her cheek in his right hand. "I like burgers. Burgers are good. Don't you like burgers?"

"Yes."

"Okay, then. Burgers it is. We'll save the fancy food for another night."

Gaia smiled, happy Will was acknowledging that there would be a next time.

Will

Why are we doomed to repeat the bad moments? Sometimes it feels like we're trapped in the same suck-ass storylines over and over, like reruns of a lame sitcom.

Sitting here, stuffing my face with home fries, I'm overwhelmed with a sense of déjà vu. I've played this part before. At first I couldn't place it, but then I saw the Sox pennant on the wall and remembered. . . .

It was the end of spring, and my Little League team was having its final game. We'd gone undefeated the entire season—due in large part, I might add, to a pretty awesome hitting streak I was on. It was a huge deal, not just for me, but also for the entire community. In fact, half the town was planning on coming. But not my mother.

Mom had gotten the chance to earn some extra cash doing inventory for a local department store. She accepted the job knowing full well that the work was scheduled the same weekend as my game. With Mom busy and Uncle Casper off on one of his fishing trips, that left me—one of the team's star players—with no one to cheer me on at the game. It was an awful feeling. Simultaneously angry and hurt and skittish. I even considered pretending to be sick on game day.

Luckily Mom was dating Bob Bentley at the time, and he offered to take me. It was really nice of him, and I was really getting close to the guy, but for some reason, I still didn't play my best. I guess I couldn't quite shake off that feeling of being shunted aside in order to really concentrate on the game.

Luckily we still won, and Bob and I celebrated by eating massive amounts of junk food.

Later that night I heard him and my mom fighting. I can still replay it now almost word for word—as if it wore grooves in my brain matter. I remember Bob's low yet calm voice telling Mom that she should have been there, that she needed to make me her top priority. Then Mom fired back that I *was* her top priority, that she was earning money to make sure I had food to eat, which was more important than a silly baseball game. The whole thing went on for over an hour—it was the beginning of the end for the two of them.

Right now I have the same heavy sensation in my gut that I had then—the same boyish need for attention.

I don't know where this relationship with Gaia is going. I'm doing my damnedest to make things work out, but I don't think she's giving it her best effort. I'm not sure where I fall on her overall list of priorities, but I strongly suspect it isn't in the top three.

There's no doubt in my mind that Gaia is the one for me. She can make things better. Sometimes things are so perfect between us—our secret e-mails, our soul-baring conversation while trapped in the courthouse, and our incredible night of passion at the motel. But those moments are so few. Stuff always seems to muscle in between us, and I'm getting damn tired of it.

So here I go again. Begging for attention. Pouting because the FBI is keeping her away from me. Maybe I just need to get over it. Maybe I should swallow my ego whole and realize that I may never come first with her, no matter how involved we get.

But maybe I can't.

Gaia grunted in frustration and slammed shut a kitchen drawer, causing the old, rickety trailer to rock slightly on its blocks.

"Take it easy," Kim warned. "No mishandling evidence."

"I'm sorry. It's just . . ." She closed her eyes and pressed her fingertips to her forehead. "I feel like there's something we're overlooking."

They'd spent over an hour already going through Terrell's belongings, but so far all they'd uncovered was that he had the housekeeping abilities of a three-toed sloth and a penchant for soft porn.

Kim, being a pathological neat freak, was finding it hard to be there. To him the trashed-out trailer was almost as revolting as a grisly murder scene. How anyone could actually exist in such a place was beyond his comprehension. Clothes so dirty they seemed to be in an advanced state of decay. Piles of smelly dishes growing new life-forms in the sink. Apparently when he ran out of dishes, Terrell just started eating right out of cans and then left them lying around. One was still half full of some sort of chili—its remaining contents petrified into a solid block, the spoon cemented inside.

It had looked bad in the beginning when Terrell ran off after Gaia found the knit cap and sweater. But Terrell, of course, was denying any involvement in the murders. He'd said he was out stealing on the nights of the killings, but he couldn't exactly prove it. It wasn't like thieves punched a time card. And Kim's instincts just weren't buzzing the way they normally did when he was following a lead.

At first it had been refreshing to be partnered with Gaia after Will. Not that Will was horrible, but he had been somewhat sloppy in his attention to detail. At times he was even unfocused to the point where Kim started to doubt his commitment to standard investigative procedure. (Although to be fair, Gaia *had* just gone AWOL and Will had seemed to be suffering a severe case of withdrawal.)

With Gaia, however, he was having the opposite problems. She was almost *too* focused. He wished she would forget the details. She seemed so determined to examine every blade of grass that she couldn't step back and get the wider view.

Kim pushed himself to a standing position and dusted off his pants. He was going to need a long shower when they got back to Quantico. "Gaia, we've been over every squalid inch of this place," he said, rolling down his sleeves. "There's nothing here."

"Maybe we should try to speak to more of the neighbors," she said.

Kim stifled a groan. They had spent two hours talking to the other residents of the trailer park—those who would cooperate. Most of them simply slammed their doors in their faces or yelled through their window screens to leave them the hell alone.

"Gaia, stop." Kim held up a hand as if pushing her words back into her face. "Listen to yourself. You're convinced he did it simply because you hate him for hurting Kelly."

Gaia shook her head. "That's not true. I mean, it's true, but it's not the whole story. Come on. You've got to admit he's the strongest lead we have so far. We know he can be dangerous to women, we know he's committed crimes, and we know he either made contact or tried to make contact with the three victims through the dating service. Plus he's stalking his ex-wife. That's a lot."

"But a lot of things also don't fit," he pointed out. "For one thing, he isn't left-handed. Also, he's smaller and weaker than the estimated height and strength of the assailant. And to tell you the truth, I don't think he fits the psych profile at all. He's not smart enough to be the killer or brazen enough. Terrell is a skittish simpleton—a slob and a chauvinist pig, but he's not a calculating murderer."

"That's your opinion," Gaia grouched. She snatched a framed, grime-stained photograph off the windowsill and stared at it. Peering over her shoulder, Kim could see it was a picture of Jasmine as a baby. "I've got to be *sure*, Kim. Otherwise I'd never forgive myself."

Kim felt bad for her. He knew how important this was to Gaia. She was so intent on stopping the lollipop murderer and determined to prevent Terrell from hurting Kelly and Jasmine. But somehow she was getting the two goals confused—combining them into one overarching mission. Why did she feel so responsible for Kelly and Jasmine? Gaia seemed to be powered by a compulsive, unconscious need. But for what? What sorts of demons was this dredging up for her?

"Well, until you *are* sure, we owe it to these women to look at additional suspects."

He watched as Gaia stared down at the photo of Jasmine. Her

right index finger made a circular, tracing motion over the little girl's frozen, smiling face. Then, slowly and deliberately, she set the picture on the counter and stalked out the door into the breezy sunshine.

LEET-SPEAK

Gaia and Kim found Lyle in the bowels of the bureau lab, buzzing along with all the high-tech equipment.

"I didn't believe you at first. I mean, anyone this techno-savvy should be flaunting this in all the chat rooms," he said, patting the laptop as if it were a dutiful pet.

Gaia had no idea what he was talking about, but it seemed to be good.

"So . . . you found something?" she asked.

"The data-mining application Catherine told you about. It's here! Well, not the application exactly, but I found her notes on how to build it."

"Her notes?"

"Yeah. To herself. It was all coded, like you said. It's amazing, really." He turned the laptop toward him and began clacking on its keyboard like a virtuoso pianist. "Here's the brilliant part. Instead of painstakingly browsing all the files, I simply tried to compile the entire program and the debugger puked when it hit a line of leet-speak."

Gaia's brow furrowed. "Leet-speak?"

"Programmer slang. Our own pig Latin. All I had to do was follow it. See? Here it is."

Gaia squinted at the typing on the screen.

```
#!/u5r/81N/p3rl -w
#
# cH04/3RR0R/EX1: 5m@LL 3X@Mpl3 U51N9 M@nuAL 3rR0R
Check1N9.

u$3 DBI; # L0@D +H3 d81 M0DUI3

### PERPH0rM +3h C0NNEc+10N u51ng +H3 0R4cl3 dR1v3R
MY $DBH = DB1->c0NN3c+( uNd3pH, "$+0N35", "$t0N35", {
pR1n+3RR0R => 0,
R41s33RR0R => 0
} ) 0r D13 "C4N'+ C0NN3c+ to Th3 d4t48453: $dB1::3RR5+r\N";

### pR3P@R3 4 $QL 5T@+3m3N+ pHOr 3xECUT10N
mY $$+h = $dBH->PR3P4R3( "$3L3C+ * PhrOM ME94li+H5" )
0r D13 "c4N'+ Pr3p4R3 $ql $+4TeM3N+: $d81::3RR5+R\N";
```

"I'm confused." Kim shook his head. "What exactly did you find?"

Lyle looked at them like they were still in diapers. "This is it. Her directions on how to get it running. All I have to do is finish deciphering it and build it. Then we can input all the Lollipop Case facts and see what it turns up."

"Yesss!" Gaia reached forward and hugged him around the neck. "Lyle, you are my man!" When she let go, a pink tinge had spread across his cheeks.

"Oh. Well, ah . . . okay. Thanks. I mean . . . you're welcome."

"Yeah, Lyle. We really appreciate your hard work," Kim said, stepping forward to shake his hand. "I'm not exactly sure what all this is, but it's clear you're doing an excellent job."

"So how long will it take for you to get it going?" Gaia asked.

Lyle shrugged. "Hard to know. Could be a day. Could be a few days. It depends."

She placed a hand on his arm. "You'll make this your top priority, right?"

"Of course." He smiled down at her. "Anything for . . . um, your case. I'll get started right away."

"Great." Gaia turned to leave, followed by Kim. "Please call me as soon as you know something," she called over her shoulder. "Work as fast and hard as you can."

"Don't worry." Lyle clapped his palms and rubbed them together. "I can't wait to put this baby together and take her for a test drive."

THE BITTER TASTE

Teenage Mutant Ninja Turtles. Michaelangelo, Leonardo, Donatello, and . . . who was the other one? Oh, yeah. Rafael.

Kim was supposed to be concentrating on the contents of the evidence boxes on the table in front of him. But instead he found himself transfixed by a photo he'd found among Terri Barker's items. It was a snapshot of her with her son, Kevin. She was kneeling beside him, her left arm slung around his slender shoulders.

Both of them were smiling gigantically. But what caught Kim's attention was the design on the T-shirt the boy was wearing—the Teenage Mutant Ninja Turtles in a group fighting stance.

Kim had also been into them as a boy. In fact, he hadn't realized that kids today even knew who they were. Maybe they were enjoying a resurgence of popularity. Or maybe the shirt was an old hand-me-down.

For some reason, Kim couldn't stop staring at Kevin in his shirt. It was one of those shaky moments when he felt crushed by the feebleness of humanity and the magnitude of their job. This boy could have been himself fifteen years ago, when he put so much faith in adults and dreamed of being as cool and strong as Spider-Man. Did this boy still adore superheroes? Or had seeing his mother die from a slash wound to the neck left him too jaded and shattered to believe in anyone again—including real people?

"Kim? You on earth?" Gaia's worried voice cut through his thoughts.

He glanced up and blinked his present surroundings into view. He was still in the evidence room. Four cardboard crates sat on the table before him, each one full of the personal effects of a lollipop murder victim. After a backlog of a few days, forensics had finally released them.

It depressed him to see four lives boiled down to these essentials. Hair samples, soil samples, a few personal items, and several grisly sketches and photos. In each case forensics had dusted and vacuumed and compared everything with the control samples. But in each case they'd found the same thing: no fingerprints, no unidentifiable hairs, and no new DNA. Just a few dark woolen fibers.

If only this picture could talk. If only it could tell us what we needed to know.

"It's sad, isn't it?" Gaia said, studying him sympathetically.

"Yeah." He carefully placed the photo back inside its bag and lifted another bag out of the crate. "It just hits me now and then. This is real. It's not a Hogan's Alley simulation but a *real* case involving *real* lives."

"I know," she said, still watching him warily. "We can take a break, if you like."

Kim shook his head. "No. I'll be fine."

He didn't want Gaia to think he couldn't handle this. Besides, it had been his idea to come here in the first place. He hadn't wanted to wait for Lyle to get Catherine's application going—if he even could. Rather than anticipate new evidence that might or might not be coming, it made sense for them to go back over what they already had.

Focus, he told himself. *You want to help that boy? Then concentrate on what you're doing.*

He pulled a stack of mail out of a wide plastic evidence bag. According to the crime scene photos, the envelopes had been heaped on a table not far from where the body lay. Sure enough, quite a few of them were covered with tiny rust-red droplets. Kim shuddered slightly as he pictured the blood spraying from Terri Barker's severed carotid artery.

Swallowing back the bitter taste in his mouth, he focused on the items themselves: this month's edition of *Ladies' Home Journal*, a gas bill, a grocery store circular, a flyer advertising a home security system . . . Kim noted the irony and continued sifting through the stack. His fingers stopped when they hit a square, soft-pink envelope.

What's this? he wondered. It looked like some sort of greeting card addressed to Terri but with no return address. He lifted the flap and slid out a colorful card. On the front cover was a photo of a rainbow arching across a waterfall. The paper itself was warped slightly, its corners softened as if it had been handled many times.

Kim opened it up. Instead of a preprinted message, someone had written out a brief note in jagged scrawl. A chill settled over him as he read it.

> *"Ecstasy! My pulse, as yours, doth temperately keep time, and makes as healthful music!"* —Shakespeare
> *Looking forward to our special evening!*

"Gaia, look at this." He handed her the card. Gaia's forehead puckered as she glanced down at the message.

"You know, there was a card with Ann's effects, too. I wonder . . ." She replaced a bagged hairbrush in the crate in front of her and lifted out a large bag of mail. Digging through the contents, she soon removed a similar dusty pink envelope. Gaia pulled out the card—with the same soft-focus photo of a waterfall on the front—and read the inside.

"It's the exact same message!" she said, her voice rising.

She set the card down and immediately dove into the next box. Sure enough, another card had been bagged with Laurel Halliday's personal effects. All were blank cards with the waterfall picture on the front. And all of them contained the exact same handwritten quote and message, minus a signature.

Kim felt a swelling sensation inside his chest. His gloved hands shook as he grasped Laurel's card—which also showed signs of wear and tear from much handling.

"This is big, Gaia. This has to be from *him*. It means he was dating them—or at least planning to."

She nodded, looking rather calm considering their big find. "But what does it mean, exactly?" she asked, frowning at the wall behind him. "Why the card? Why the quote?"

Kim opened the card and reread it. "Shakespeare. Maybe from one of his poems? Sounds like the guy was just trying to impress the women."

Gaia shook her head. "No. The quote is from *Hamlet*. From the end of act three, when Hamlet is telling his mother he isn't crazy. In Elizabethan English, 'ecstasy' meant 'madness.' It's right after he stabs Polonius to death."

"Stabs?" Kim repeated. He glanced sideways, trying to recall the play. They had studied it in high school, and he vaguely remembered the premise. Obviously Gaia had a better brain for literature than he did.

But what he lacked in literary analysis, he more than made up for in his psychological skills. Not that it took an expert to see the parallels between these murders and a reference to a play with stabbing deaths and a mother character.

"He's foreshadowing what's to come!" Kim said. "It's a warning—a warning none of the women picked up on!"

"It's worse than that," Gaia countered. "In the scene Hamlet goes on to reproach his mother. He tells her she has sinned horribly and can never be cured of her moral sickness." She held out Ann's card at arm's length, her features twisting in a look of repugnance. "This guy is scolding them and hinting at how he will punish them. He's taunting them."

Kim slowly sank into a nearby chrome-and-vinyl chair. Suddenly things were starting to make a little bit of sense—like when two puzzle pieces came together to make a more complete picture. They still had a lot of holes to fill in, but at least they were getting closer to a motive.

The killer feels these women have sinned in some way. Who the hell is this guy who quotes Shakespeare to women before slitting their throats?

One thing was pretty clear: he couldn't be Terrell Mitchum. Kim considered pointing out to Gaia that Terrell didn't seem the type to quote classic literature but decided against it.

"So we know he was in contact with the victims before killing them," Gaia said, pacing back and forth in front of the table. "So what if he didn't just mail them letters? What if he also e-mailed them? Or phoned them?"

"All e-mail goes through the dating service, and we've already looked through the victims' archives," Kim explained. "There was nothing out of the ordinary."

"What about phone records? If he requested their profile from Second Chance and was granted it, he would have received their phone numbers too."

Kim stood up and rifled through a few boxes. "This is unbelievable. I don't think Bell Atlantic ever sent them to us. It must have been an oversight." An oversight only a rookie would make.

"Then we've got to get those phone records. Today. Let's put the evidence back and see about getting a subpoena." Gaia began rebagging items and returning them to their respective boxes.

"Wait," Kim said. "Let me keep one of the cards. There's something I want to check."

He unearthed Terri Barker's card from the pile and held it up, turning it left and right as he squinted at the message once again.

The handwriting. There was a clue there; he just knew it. For one thing, it was textbook psychotic with its jagged notches and crazy angles, but something else about it bothered him.

Something about the penmanship seemed almost . . . familiar.

a rush of warmth

Okay. So it had been fifteen minutes since Gaia was supposed to show up at Le Petite—the nicest restaurant in town, where the average entrée rivaled an entire week's pay. No big deal. Something must have happened.

Like . . . maybe she suddenly doubled over with that stomach flu that had been going around? Or maybe there was a lockdown after some kook called in a bomb threat?

Or maybe she forgot?

Will sipped sparkling water from a delicate glass and checked his reflection in a sterling silver butter knife. He searched the elegant gold room for someone with long lemony hair, a short black cocktail dress, and a purposeful stride. But once again, there was no one remotely Gaia-like in view.

He checked his watch again. Eighteen minutes late.

His jaw clenched, and his insides felt like they were set to simmer. For some reason, fifteen minutes was still acceptable, but eighteen minutes took him straight to pissed off.

He should be used to it. So many times growing up, he was last one to be picked up at camp or ball practice. He could still remember how he'd punch his glove impatiently while the dusk deepened overhead. His mom always had the same ready excuse, too: *Something came up at work.* It wasn't that he doubted her; he just got tired of it. And he daydreamed about a time when she would grab her car keys and announce to her co-workers, "This will have to wait. I need to go get my boy."

Nineteen minutes.

The waiter passed for the fourth time, asking if Will was ready to order. He dismissed him with a wave of his hand.

Twenty minutes. *Damn!*

Forget it. He was tired of playing it cool. He wanted answers.

Will yanked his cell phone out of his belt holster and angrily punched up Gaia's number.

Gaia answered on the first ring. "Agent Moore." She sounded out of breath.

"Gaia? Where are you?" he whispered in a hushed voice.

"I'm just handing my keys to the valet. Why?"

He took a deep breath, trying to ignore the squeezing sensation in his gut. "It's just that . . . I was worried. I've been waiting over twenty minutes and wondered what happened to you." Will winced at the whiny-puppy pitch to his voice. *But so what?* he told himself. He wanted her to know what she was putting him through.

"Will . . . I'm so sorry I'm late, but something came up. We just got a big breakthrough," she went on.

There was a pause. Will could hear a shuffling noise followed by the maitre d's voice in the background. So something had come up. Again. For once why couldn't she just say, "This will have to wait. I've got a hot date with my boyfriend"?

"Will?" Gaia's voice was suddenly louder than the tinny reception of his cell phone.

He looked up. Gaia's smiling face greeted him warmly as she dipped into the seat across from him. She wore a black dress that hugged every curve of her athletic frame. A wash of gloss high-lighted the natural berry shade of her lips. Her golden hair was swept up, with a few stray wisps tickling her collarbone.

Will clicked off his phone and reholstered it. He was over-come with a rush of warmth that ignited him from the tips of his toes to the top of his head. He reached across the table for Gaia with one hand and signaled for the waiter with the other.

I JUST WANTED US

Dinner was delicious. Steak, medium rare, with peppercorn sauce for each. Whipped mashed potatoes for Will, vegetable medley for Gaia, and a basket of buttermilk biscuits. There had been some polite and measured chitchat during the main course, but by the time two slices of flourless chocolate cake arrived at the table, the conversation had started to flow more easily. It was a testimony to the power of comfort food.

"I'm sorry if I've been out of it lately," he said, pushing another morsel onto his fork. "I haven't let myself get close to someone in a long time."

"Me neither," she admitted, through chocolaty bites.

"Yeah, but you aren't scared," he grumbled.

Gaia was beginning to wish she hadn't told Will about her big biological secret. Sometimes it seemed like he resented her for it.

He avoided eye contact. "I guess I just have trust issues. I'm sure it's all very textbook. Probably stems from not having a dad."

"You think so?"

Will shrugged. "It's probably what Lau would say." He

unfolded then refolded his napkin. "When I was growing up, my mom had boyfriend after boyfriend." The sunlight illuminated the pensive creases on his face. "Each time I thought I'd be getting a father. I started realizing our family was different. I just wanted us to be normal."

Gaia nodded. She understood such feelings. As a child, she had always been aware of how abnormal she was compared to other kids. Even though she told herself it didn't bother her, deep down she'd always harbored a secret wish to lead a regular, dull existence. Hence her many attempts to assimilate fear into her genetic makeup.

"I remember this one guy she went out with," Will went on. "His name was Bob Bentley. Unlike the others, he really got to know me and hung out with me. When she sent him packing, I was crushed. To me he would have been the perfect dad, but my mom said he was too 'dark,' maybe just because he'd been in the military. For a long time afterward I wondered where he was and whether he still thought about me. I even fantasized about running away and finding him."

He paused, and his eyes focused on something across the dining room. Will seemed suddenly to be a young adolescent, lonely for a father as he faced his own looming manhood. Gaia felt a deep stab of sympathy.

"Anyway . . ." Will shook his head lightly, a grown-up, tired expression returning to his features. "That's when I gave up hoping and learned to protect myself. From then on, I just automatically pulled away whenever I started to feel for someone."

Again Gaia nodded. How many times had she purposefully distanced herself from people she cared about? She'd always believed that it was for the best, that she was keeping them safe from the danger that always surrounded her—but really she'd been shielding her own feelings just as much.

"I was the same way," Gaia admitted. "*Am* the same way. All through my teen years I crafted a super-strong loner image. I put up the illusion of not needing anyone ever. That way I wouldn't get hurt when they took off."

"Yeah. Exactly what I did. Still do." At last he turned and looked at her directly, and the creases on his brow smoothed slightly.

"Maybe that's why we're so competitive with each other," Gaia pointed out. "We're so much alike."

"And maybe that's why the chemistry is so great?" His mouth tilted in a crooked smile, simultaneously shy and mischievous.

"So . . . what happens now?" she asked. "With us?"

Will's smile extended and he raised his water glass. "We do what feels right."

SENSING TROUBLE

Gaia flipped another page in *Serial Murderers: A Thirty-Year Overview*, slid down her headboard, and let out a belch. Along with a bloated belly and her blistered feet (she never wore heels for a reason!), it was yet another reminder of her wonderful dinner with Will.

Wonderful, except for her wandering mind. It seemed like the second they reached the parking lot, her attention had shifted back to the Lollipop Case. The discovery of the greeting cards was big. It meant they were on the trail, getting a sense of the killer and his motives. But she was so thankful for taking even a small break for some long-overdue quality time together with Will. It was as close to a normal date as two FBI agents-in-training could get. And he would have come back to her room if he hadn't had a late seminar with Special Agent Crowley on the older agent's deep-cover work inside the Chicago mob.

A knock sounded on the door—light yet musical. It had to be Kim and his classically trained hands.

"Come in," she called out, still too fatigued by digestion to get off her butt.

The door opened and Kim's bristly hairdo poked around the edge, followed by his face. "Gaia?" he said, his features cramped and tentative looking. "Can I talk to you for a sec?"

Gaia sat forward, instantly sensing trouble. "Sure. What is it?"

Kim stepped into the room and shut the door, keeping his hands behind his back. "I need to tell you something," he said. "But you've got to promise me you'll hear me out before you say or do anything."

"Okay, fine," she said with a shrug. "I promise."

His eyebrows lifted doubtfully.

Gaia sighed impatiently. "Really. I swear I'll hear you out." She placed one hand over her heart and lifted the other in a rudimentary oath-taking gesture.

"Okay." Kim took a few steps forward and moved his right arm out from behind him. In his hand he held one of the Lollipop Killer's cards, still in its protective sheath. "I hope you don't mind, but I had the handwriting analyzed."

She exhaled in relief. Was that it? He was afraid she'd be mad that he took this step without consulting her? "That's great," she said, hoping to put him at ease. "I was going to suggest that myself." She grinned at him. *See? Not mad.*

"The graphology revealed pretty much what we would expect," he said. "Intense rage, aggressive tendencies, possible split personality. But . . . that wasn't all. I also think I might have found a handwriting match." He paused, half cringing.

"A match? That's fantastic!" Why was he looking at her that way? Did he think she'd accuse him of hogging all the glory? "Well? Who is it?"

At this point Kim brought forward his left hand, which held a few sheets of paper clipped together with a large metal brad. "The sample on top," he said, pointing.

Gaia frowned. The two sets of writing looked completely different to her. "Are you sure?"

He nodded. "Look closely. The size and tilt of the writing is different, as is the legibility, but the letters are formed almost identically. Same spacing between words and lines. Same letter connections. Same concealing strokes. The analysis confirms it." He reached over and flipped to the page underneath. "See? There's a seventy-six percent chance that the two samples were written by the same person—perhaps one by the right hand and one by the left, which would explain the differences."

A creeping numbness spread through Gaia's limbs. She really didn't like where this was going.

"This other sample," she said croakily. "It reminds me of the ones we did for class that day."

"It is." Kim's face drooped sadly. "It's Will's."

Gaia shook her head. "You're insane," she said through pursed lips.

"Gaia, listen to me." Kim took a step forward and looked her right in the eye. "I know you don't want to hear this, but you have to. There are too many coincidences here. We know Will can use his left hand, he's the same and build and strength as the killer, and there's a high probability his handwriting is a match. Plus . . ." He paused and hunched his shoulders guiltily. "I checked the Quantico entry and exit logs. Will was off campus every time there was a murder."

"You can't be serious! This is Will! You *know* him. You've *worked* with him."

A wounded expression crept over Kim's face. "I don't like this any more than you do," he said in a low voice. "It's just that there are too many similarities. Right now it's the most logical explanation we have."

"But it's *not* logical," she pleaded, "Will is dedicating his life to saving people. He could never do such terrible things. Why would he?"

"I don't know. But if we delve a little deeper—"

"No. *You* need to delve deeper. I knew there was friction between you and Will, but I had no idea it was this bad. I never dreamed you'd stoop this low to get back at him."

Kim flinched as if she'd just slapped him. "Gaia. You have to trust me. All I'm doing is—"

She stalked right up next to him and pointed to the door. "Get out of my room before I throw you out the window," she hissed.

For a moment Kim just stood there gazing at her with a sad, defeated look. Then he turned and loped dejectedly toward the door.

As soon as he set his hand on the knob, he straightened suddenly, as if bolstered by some newfound strength.

"I know it's hard to think of Will this way," he said, turning to face her again. "But think about what happened with Catherine. There were probably clues all around us that she wasn't what she pretended to be, but we refused to see them. Well, I'm not going to let anyone else fool me, fool *us*, again."

"Get . . ." Gaia's chest heaved with deep, fuming breaths. *"Out!"*

"Twenty-four hours, Gaia," he said, staring back at her stubbornly, although his voice wavered slightly. "I want to be double sure of everything before telling anyone else. But we have a responsibility to come forward with this. I'm going to take one more day to go over the facts and follow up any new leads. Afterward, if the evidence is still this strong, we have to go to Malloy and Bishop." He held her gaze for a second longer and then disappeared through the door into the hall.

Gaia stood stiff as steel, glaring at the air that previously held Kim. *Let him threaten,* she told herself. *He doesn't have a leg to stand on.* If anything, perhaps his going to Bishop and Malloy would convince them that he couldn't handle the pressures of the case. They would see how off base he was in an instant.

Or would they?

Kim could make it sound really convincing—or at least alarming enough that they would interrogate Will and watch him closely for the rest of his training. And knowing Will and his billowing pride, it just couldn't happen. He'd already suffered the humiliation of being reprimanded and taken off the Lollipop Case. Any more embarrassment would do him in.

"I have to do something," she said with a decisive nod.

If only she knew what that *something* was.

Where was it? Where the hell had she put it?

Gaia dumped the contents of her briefcase onto her bed and began rummaging through the assortment of files, handbooks, loose papers, and peanut M&M wrappers. Finally she unearthed a fat stack of printouts held together by a jumbo binder clip—the Second Chance dating service profiles. Picking up the stack, she climbed onto Catherine's former bed and huddled in the corner, ready to work.

If Kim was determined to think of Will as a knife-wielding killer, that was his own business. But she had just as much right to *disprove* his theory. She could comb through the case materials and extract any nuggets of information proving Will couldn't have done what Kim said. And it made sense to start with the dating service. If she could demonstrate to their superiors that they had just as much so-called evidence on other people, then she could show this was all just a big mistake.

"Yes! Here we are." Gaia lifted out the sheets they'd painstakingly separated from the main stack a couple of days ago—profiles of people who seemed slightly suspicious. Kim had continued to investigate them after Terrell was arrested, and his notes were all over the pages. Apparently the left-handed pitcher had moved out of the area a month ago. The scary misogynist had presided over a Bible class on the nights of two of the four murders. Three of the avid fishermen also had iron-clad alibis, and the fourth was in a wheelchair. That left only one fisherman—only according to Kim's findings there had been a mistake on the form. The fisher "man" was actually a five-foot-one woman.

This was bad. What happened to all their potential suspects? Now she had to start all over again with the main stack.

"I know you're here somewhere," she mumbled as she quickly flipped the pages, creating a slight breeze that pushed the loose hairs off her face. Somewhere in the pile was a big, strong, left-handed freak with a deep hatred toward women and a penchant for Shakespeare.

What . . . that's it! She had new info to scan for. Now that they'd uncovered the cards and their message, she should check for anyone with a literary or theater background.

She decided to begin with the half stack that Kim had pored through last time. *Let's see . . .* Aaron Abrahmson liked to read, but exclusively Tolkien. Still, she pulled him from the stack. The next guy had nothing suspicious listed—ditto the next twenty. Just typical, lonely single or divorced men trying to impress prospective dates with important-sounding job titles or references to their restored Trans Ams.

Gaia let out a grunt of frustration and flipped a page. Her eyes glanced over the name. Cold prickles spread over her. *Bob Bentley?* Wasn't that the name of the man Will said his mom used to date? She examined the rest of the profile but found no other identifying data. *Maybe it's just a coincidence?*

But what if it wasn't? What if this was the exact same guy? Didn't Will say his mom broke up with him because he was too "dark"?

The prickles were still there, as big as icicles, warning her. Gaia had an overwhelming hunch they needed to check this man out. In her experience, people from the past didn't just pop up for no reason. There was always a motive—and too often it was a twisted one. She pressed the printout to her chest and bounced off the bed, heading for the door. Kim needed to hear this.

She paused in mid-step. Or not.

What if Kim only saw this as further evidence of Will's guilt? What if he assumed Will was in collusion with this long-lost father figure? Or that he'd adopted Bob's identity as a cover?

No. She shouldn't trust him. And besides, Will had told her about Bob Bentley in confidence, after a very intimate evening. He had never shared inner memories and secrets with her before, but all that had changed. When they had been trapped inside the courthouse, he had let down the force field he maintained at all times and really, truly opened himself up to her. The end result was incredible—an emotional link that was deeper and more intense than any she had ever experienced before.

She couldn't betray him by telling Kim. She'd have to turn to someone else for help.

Retrieving her cell phone from her dresser, she flipped it open and quickly punched in a number. "Hello, Lyle? It's Gaia."

"Gaia! I'm so glad you called. I'm going to have that application up and running in a matter of hours. Possibly by midday tomorrow."

"Really? That's fantastic!"

"Sorry it's taking a while," he added. "I would have had the program up sooner, but I misinterpreted some of the code. I had assumed her word *void* meant 'zero' when it actually meant 'null.'"

"Yeah? Well, that's understandable," Gaia said, even though she had no idea what he was talking about. "Listen, can I tear you away from that for just one moment? I need another favor."

"I guess so." Lyle sounded a little disappointed. "But I thought this was my top priority."

"It is, but I need another favor. Don't worry, it's a quick one. Piece of virtual cake for someone with your talent. But if you're busy, I could call someone else."

"No, no. It's fine," he quickly replied. "What is it?"

"I need an address for a guy named Bob Bentley. Check the expanded local listings. I don't have a number or age or anything. All I know is that he used to be in the military and he possibly lived in South Carolina during the late eighties, early nineties. Can you check for me and call me back?"

"I'm on it."

"Oh, and Lyle? One more thing."

"Yeah?"

"Please don't say anything to Kim about this, okay? He's, um . . . really stressed right now, and I'm trying to shoulder some of his load. So make sure you call me with the information only."

"Right. I'm your guy."

She disconnected the phone and heaved a sigh, feeling a strange gripping sensation in her gut.

Here she was again, *not* following FBI protocol. And it could very well be the last strike that would get her tossed out. But she had no time for protocol. Lives were at stake, and now Will's future was on the line.

Will had risked everything to help her when she went AWOL. Now it was time for her to return the favor. So she had to do it her way. This was a job for Loner Gaia. For sneaky, rule-bending Gaia.

For *Will's* Gaia.

A MATTER OF LIFE AND DEATH

> *K.—*
>
> *Something came up. Go get the phone records without me. I'll try to call later.*
>
> *G.*

Kim crumpled up the note Gaia had pushed beneath his door and climbed out of the FBI-issue Impala. He straightened his collar and tightened his blazer around him, shielding himself from the chill. Strong ocean winds were pushing through, refrigerating the morning air and pushing thick, chewy clouds over the sun.

At least the weather fit his mood. He'd been in a dull, depressed funk ever since he'd confronted Gaia with his suspicions. It wasn't like he'd expected it to go well, but he hadn't banked on feeling like such a villain. Gaia's defending of Will was understandable. They were clearly in love—or at least the wiggy, feverish stages of prelove. But he had hoped to appeal to Gaia's logical side, to the clearheaded investigator inside her. As hard as it must have been to think of Will as a killer, Gaia should have been able to acknowledge the unsettling amount of parallels he'd found.

As Kim approached the front doors of the Bell Atlantic building, he caught sight of his reflection in the glass. He looked shriveled and concave, weakened by guilt and a long, sleepless night.

Gaia should be here, he grumbled inwardly. *I shouldn't have to do this myself.*

But she wasn't here. He had to suck it up and do his job. Having always been partnered with such strong personality types, it was easy to hang back and hide behind them. Gaia and Will were born to be commanding, firm, and somewhat imposing. But Kim wasn't sure he could convincingly pull it off without them. Even though he felt fully trained and capable, he still couldn't quite shake off the notion that he was a child playing dress-up instead of a real-life FBI agent.

As he took the final few steps toward the entrance, Kim straightened his necktie and smoothed his hastily styled hair. Then he threw back his shoulders, took a breath, and pushed through the door.

The lobby was bright and noisy. Buzzing fluorescents cast a yellow light on the white walls and dingy white floor. Across from the entrance was a broad expanse of wall with closed doors on both ends and an open area cut in the middle, like a bar or puppet theater. A half-dozen people were already in line, waiting their turn to see the woman at the counter. A nearby sign listed several helpful facts such as the company's hours of operation, documents needed to open an account, and special phone numbers for those needing technical assistance (although Kim couldn't figure out exactly *how* people could call for service if their phones didn't work). Unfortunately there were no helpful hints for newly knighted FBI agents with subpoenas.

Am I supposed to wait in line? Kim wondered.

Probably not. Anyone with a badge could most likely forgo all etiquette and cut right to the front. It was what Gaia would have done. And besides, this was genuinely a matter of life and death.

Kim raised his chin to what he hoped was an authoritative angle and strode to the head of the line. The clerk at the window was helping a man dressed head to toe in Civil War–era military garb, complete with frock coat and kepi.

"But I know they're there. I can hear them breathing," the man was saying to the woman.

"Sir, I assure you. There is no one listening in on your phone line."

"Excuse me." Kim leaned forward and held up his identification card. "I'm Agent Kim Lau, Federal Bureau of Investigation. Whom can I speak with about obtaining a set of phone records for local numbers? I need them immediately."

The man and the female clerk gave him matching incredulous stares. "Um . . . my supervisor, Mr. Lowry, can help you, sir," the woman said. "I'll find him for you."

"Thank you."

After the woman trotted away, Kim leaned against the counter, nodding politely at the Civil War re-enactor.

The man tipped his cap and then leaned closer to Kim. "You guys aren't listening in on me, are you?" he asked in a whisper.

Thankfully the woman returned at that moment with a tall, thin, mustached man.

"I'm Dan Lowry," the man said, shaking Kim's hand. He gestured at the door to the left. "If you would like to come back to our servicing area, I can help you with what you need."

As Kim walked toward the side door, he glanced back at the

people in the lobby. They were all watching him with something bordering on awe. He held back a grin. Local eccentrics notwithstanding, it felt good to be treated with so much respect. He even felt different—like he'd morphed into a super-version of himself. Without the badge and shoulder holster he was a mild-mannered bookworm. With them he was agent guy, able to cut lines and demand cooperation and draw reverent glances wherever he went.

But I'm also duty-bound to protect all these people, he reminded himself.

And hopefully he would. With any luck Mr. Lowery would give him the numbers that would lead him to their killer—be it Will or someone else.

But at least he'd already proved one thing. He'd proved to himself that he could do this after all. Suddenly he didn't have to pretend anymore.

SOMEONE'S HERE

Here it is. 1402 Dewberry Lane. Gaia pulled the blue Cavalier in front of a redbrick, ranch-style home. According to Lyle, this Lake Ridge address was the only local listing for one Bob Bentley, retired navy electrician and former resident of Greensboro, South Carolina.

She cut the engine and sat frowning through the windshield at the house. The place was modest, yet meticulously cared for. The stone walkway was bordered with cheery-looking geraniums. Robust azalea bushes flanked the front stoop. The lawn was a lush hunter green and neatly trimmed. And inside a brass bracket beside the front door, an American flag flapped in the breeze.

Even though her training had taught her to not make such assumptions, Gaia couldn't help thinking that the home seemed too cozy and well maintained to harbor a serial killer. She had expected someplace more shoddy and sinister looking. Not unlike Terrell's trailer.

The tingling vibes she'd felt when looking over Bob Bentley's profile had disappeared along with the morning mist that hugged the hills during most of her drive. She really hoped she hadn't made a mistake. She was completely out of do-overs with her superiors. Leaving a cryptic note with her partner and driving for over an hour on a wild-goose chase would *not* be a good way to earn brownie points.

Thank God it isn't my only lead, she thought as she climbed out of the car and headed up the walkway. Lyle should have the data-mining search engine up and running by now, and he'd promised to call her (and only her) when it was finished processing the case data.

Gaia rang the doorbell and stepped back, stifling a yawn. She really wished she had allowed herself a second cup of coffee, especially after a night of tossing and turning. *At least someone's here,* she told herself as she eyed the freshly waxed Lincoln in the driveway. She'd been worried she might pull up to an empty house, but she hadn't wanted to tip anyone off that she was coming either.

Sure enough, after she'd waited a few seconds, the door opened and a well-dressed, middle-aged woman stood in the frame. "Yes?" she said, giving Gaia a quizzical once-over.

"Good morning, ma'am. My name is Gaia Moore, and I'm with the Federal Bureau of Investigation," Gaia said as she flashed her ID card. "I'm looking for a Mr. Bob Bentley."

The woman's features folded into a pattern of worry lines. She leaned out of the house, glancing to the left and right, before gesturing toward the tile foyer in back of her. "Won't you please come in?"

"Thank you." As Gaia stepped inside the house, her nostrils instantly picked up the seductive aroma of fresh coffee. Her senses sharpened automatically.

The woman shut the door and spun around, fixing Gaia with an apprehensive stare. "Has Bob done something wrong?" she asked, tugging the bottom of her blue lamb's wool sweater.

Interesting, Gaia thought. The lady automatically assumed he was guilty of something. That meant she felt he was at least *capable* of committing a misdeed.

Gaia fought to keep her expression neutral. "I'm sorry . . . are you any relation to Mr. Bentley?"

"Oh, forgive me." The woman shook her head as if waking herself. "I'm Marsha Bentley, Bob's wife. Please make yourself comfortable." She motioned toward a living area full of curvy antique chairs and a toile-covered camel-back sofa. Gaia perched on one of the chairs while Mrs. Bentley sat in the middle of the sofa, nervously kneading her hands in her lap.

"Is Mr. Bentley here?" Gaia asked, glancing around at the polished wooden tables and porcelain figurines.

"Bob doesn't live here anymore."

Gaia wasn't surprised to hear it, judging by the total lack of masculine debris.

"We're separated," Mrs. Bentley went on. She stiffened slightly and kept smoothing her slacks as if dusting off invisible crumbs.

"I'm sorry," Gaia said, trying hard to remain expressionless while a new tingly feeling spread over her. The fact that Bob didn't get along well with the current woman in his life also fit neatly into the killer's profile.

"Yes, well . . . we managed to hold things together until Cindy went off to college," Mrs. Bentley went on. "But as soon as she moved out to Stanford, he moved out, too." She smiled a tight, joyless smile as if donning a mask.

"Cindy is your daughter?" Gaia asked, wanting to keep the woman talking.

Mrs. Bentley nodded. "That's right. That's her there." She pointed to a frosted glass picture frame on the table next to Gaia.

Gaia picked it up and studied the photograph. It was a family portrait taken in a department store studio. A teenage girl sat between Mrs. Bentley and a forty-something man. All three of them were wearing the same forced smile Mrs. Bentley was currently sporting for Gaia's sake. "She's beautiful," Gaia said. "And this is Mr. Bentley, I presume?"

Mrs. Bentley's face fell. "Yes. That's Bob."

Gaia stared hard at the photo, as if trying to divine its secrets. Bob Bentley wasn't a bad-looking man, with his shaggy, salt-and-pepper hair, strong Roman nose, and broad shoulders. But something about him made him appear rather aloof. Maybe it was the way he stood slightly apart from the others or the way his arms were folded across his short-sleeved henley, accentuating the colorful anchor tattoo on his right bicep.

"Turns out we shouldn't have bothered with the whole charade," Mrs. Bentley continued as she glared at the photo in Gaia's grasp. "Do you know what Cindy said when I called to tell her we'd separated? She said, 'What took you so long?' Said she couldn't understand why I put up with his nonsense as long as I did. His own daughter! She even called him a chauvinist. Her whole life she felt he'd been disappointed that she wasn't a son. Maybe she was right. I don't know. . . ." Her voice trailed off sadly.

Gaia nodded sympathetically. So Bob was a sexist jerk, huh? His own daughter felt unloved by him? It was looking more and more like she was on the right trail. At the same time, though, Gaia couldn't help feeling a little devious. The woman was obviously lonely and was using Gaia's visit as a chance to unload. Mrs. Bentley had no idea Gaia suspected her husband of three grisly murders.

Burning the image of Bob's face in her memory, Gaia carefully replaced the frame on the table beside her. The movement seemed to snap Mrs. Bentley out of her thoughts.

"I apologize for rambling on like this. You must be very busy." Her prim smile returned, as did her Stepford Wife tone. "Can I get you anything? Perhaps a cup of coffee?"

"Thank you, but I'm afraid I don't have the time," Gaia said, rising to her feet. "Do you know Mr. Bentley's current address?"

Mrs. Bentley stood along with Gaia. "He was staying with friends, but he moved out after a couple of weeks. No one's seen him much in the past month or so."

"Really? How do you know?"

"You aren't the only one who's come around looking for him. People from the bank have been, too." Her nose wrinkled disdainfully. "I'll bet anything he's laying low and living in that stinky old boat of his."

"A boat? You mean, like a fishing boat?" Gaia hoped her excitement wasn't too evident.

"Honestly, I have no idea what type of boat it is. But yes, he uses it for fishing—among other things."

Gaia pulled out her notepad and flipped it open. "Could you please tell me what marina it's docked at?"

Mrs. Bentley shook her head. "It isn't at a marina. It's at our beachfront property. Would you like me to write down directions for you?"

"Yes, please."

Mrs. Bentley walked to a stone counter that separated the living room from the dining area and began writing on a stack of floral stationery.

Gaia glanced one last time at the photo. Just like before, when she read over his profile, she felt an undeniable sense of fate.

An intense prickly feeling trilled through her, emanating from her left hip. At first she assumed it was that heavy intuition, her own freakish spidey sense telling her she was close to solving the case. But then she remembered: she had set her cell phone to vibrate.

She headed for the front door, clutching her phone. "Excuse me, Mrs. Bentley. I'm going to step outside and take this call."

Gaia stepped outside and scurried down the steps to the stone walkway. "Agent Moore speaking," she said.

"Gaia? This is Lyle."

She smiled. The guy had no need to identify himself. She'd

recognize his nasal drone anywhere. "Lyle, my man. Talk to me. What have you found out?"

"I've got good news and bad news. The good news is that Catherine's application is up and running perfectly."

"Yes! You are the man."

There came a pause.

"Lyle? You were saying about the program?"

"Uh . . . yeah. Right. It's a real work of art. I entered all the case data you gave me, and it cross-referenced it with every data bank you can think of—criminal, medical, educational, governmental—not to mention some I don't think we're legally allowed to access, even under the Patriot Act."

"Go on," she urged, tapping her foot impatiently on the stone pavers.

"Well, here's the bad news. It turned up almost nothing. The only bit of information it uncovered that we'd overlooked came from the National Weather Service. According to their records, there was moderate rainfall in the area on the night of every single murder."

"Really? That's it?"

"Yeah. I'm really sorry. I honestly thought this would be like a magic wand or something."

"That's okay, Lyle. Thanks for all of your hard work. Really."

"No problem," he said morosely. "Anytime."

Gaia turned off her phone and held it against her chest. As it turned out, she might not have needed Catherine's super–search engine after all. Bob Bentley was a misogynist and an avid fisherman who hadn't been seen much in the past several weeks.

Looked like she was well on her way to solving the case without the wonders of technology.

A JITTERY FEELING

Kim gazed out the car window at the yellow-brick strip mall. It seemed unremarkable enough—a small neighborhood drugstore, a real estate office, and a marine recruiting station. The parking lot wasn't even a quarter full. In fact, judging by all the vegetation that was thriving inside the gaping cracks in the asphalt, it looked like the shopping center rarely saw a lot of action.

Yet according to the phone company records, someone had placed a call from here to Mrs. Laurel Halliday only six hours before she was viciously murdered.

Kim climbed out of the sedan and approached the bank of pay phones that stood along the left exterior wall of the drugstore. Just four typical phones inside four typical Bell Atlantic half booths. *What am I expecting to find?* Kim wondered. *Why am I even here?*

Since the phones were outside the mall and that side of the building didn't have windows, there was no way store employees could monitor them. Kim could have had someone dust for prints, but that could turn up dozens of different sets. So unless the killer just happened to have dropped his ID card or left some confessional graffiti, there was no way to find out who had placed the call.

He had been hoping the pay phones were inside a place of business in plain sight of employees and video cameras. But it looked like the Lollipop Killer was smart enough to avoid that—choosing a phone completely out of sight of everyone.

Well . . . maybe not *everyone*.

As Kim scanned the surroundings, he noticed a lone figure in the distance. A man in faded jeans and a tattered button-down was standing at the corner of the nearby intersection, holding up a cardboard sign. As Kim walked toward him, he could make out the large, hand-scrawled message: Please Help. God Bless.

"Excuse me," Kim called out as he hiked through the grass skirting the parking lot.

The man instinctively ducked his head and lowered the sign.

"Pardon me, sir," Kim said, stopping about a foot away from the curb. "May I ask you a few questions?" He pulled out his ID card and held it up.

The man glanced at it briefly and turned away. "I didn't do nothing," he mumbled, hunching his shoulders.

"No, sir. You didn't. I simply want to ask you a few things." Kim took out his walled and extracted a ten-dollar bill.

He knew that what he was doing went against regulations. Paying a potential witness violated all sorts of laws and ethics. Yet off the record, every law enforcement official he knew understood the value of paid informants. Transients and prostitutes saw all kinds of things in their day-to-day existence on the streets that could prove useful to an investigation. But since they considered "cops" their natural enemies, it was often necessary to coax the details out of them.

It's what any detective worth his or her salt would do, Kim told himself as he dangled the bill in front of the man. *Besides, it's only ten bucks.*

The man's bleary brown eyes looked from Kim's face to the money in his outstretched hand. Kim felt a pang of pity for him. The man looked about his father's age. He was tall and his shoulders were broad, but his chest looked sunken, as if he were the abandoned shell of a once-powerful man. Kim found himself wondering what the man's story was and how he'd ended up so down on his luck.

The man snatched the money from Kim's hand, an expression of defeat weighing down his crinkled, sunburned face. "Okay," he mumbled. "What do you want?"

"Is this corner your territory?" Kim asked. From what he understood of the homeless community, panhandlers usually staked out an area as their own and no one else was allowed to beg there until the person moved on.

He nodded hesitantly.

"How long have you been at this spot?"

The man lifted his shoulders. "About five or six weeks. Not sure exactly."

Kim nodded. He imagined people who lived this way didn't monitor the passage of time as closely as others. "Do you see those phones over there?" he asked the man, gesturing across the parking lot to the side of the pharmacy.

"Yep." The man furrowed his brow as if confused.

"Since you can see them so clearly from your post, I'm wondering if you've noticed any people making calls lately."

"Some," the man replied. "Usually folks bring their own phones nowadays."

"Can you tell me if you saw anyone at those phones about eight days ago, in the early evening?"

The man lifted his chin and squinted as if thinking hard. "Well, now. I only remember two folks making calls the last week or so."

Kim felt a stirring of hope. *Maybe this was a good idea after all.* "Really? Who?"

"One was a woman pushing her baby in a stroller. I know she was having a fight with whoever she was talking to 'cause I could darn near hear her yelling all the way over here."

Kim nodded along patiently, pleased that the man seemed much less skittish around him than before. "And the other person you saw?"

"Just some guy."

"What did he look like?"

The man shook his head. "Don't know. Couldn't see his face. Big, strong guy."

"Young or old?"

"Can't rightly say."

"Can you describe what he was wearing?"

The man squinted up at the sky. "Don't recall exactly. I think pants and one of them shirts with a hood on it."

"Could it have been running clothes?"

The man shrugged. "All I saw was him walking through the lot to the phones."

"Which direction did he come from?"

"Over that way." The man turned and pointed down the road in the opposite direction of his intersection.

Toward Quantico base!

A jittery feeling came over Kim. A surge of . . . something. Excitement? Apprehension? Guilt? He couldn't quite identify it. "Can you tell me what day that was?" he asked the man, his voice high and fast.

The man squinted again. "I'd say on or around a week ago. I remember it rained that night."

By now Kim's pulse was echoing through his skull. "Thank

you, sir." Kim pulled another ten-dollar bill out of his wallet and held it out. The man took it, bowed his head in a gesture of thanks, and stalked back to his corner.

As Kim jogged back to his car, he realized his visit had basically accomplished nothing. He could never call the transient as a credible witness—especially after having paid him for his cooperation. Plus he knew he should take everything the man had told him with several grains of salt. There was just no telling just how mentally healthy he was.

Yet he still felt a heady rush of vindication.

He was on the right track—he was sure of it. Will could have come here and made the call while he was out on one of his long runs. It made perfect sense.

Now all he had to do was convince Gaia.

BLOOD WAS BLOOD

Gaia stood behind a cluster of oak trees and watched the decrepit houseboat bobbing in the surf several yards in front of her. Mrs. Bentley's map and directions had led her directly to this weedy, rocky stretch of beach only five miles from their home. Leaving her car parked along the main road, Gaia had headed down the sloping dirt drive on foot, taking cover in the dense patches of oaks and white pines that blanketed the area. She'd wanted the element of surprise, but so far the place seemed deserted.

There was a rusty Ford F-150 parked in the weeds nearby and empty cans of Pabst Blue Ribbon littered the ground. Footprints were clearly visible in the soft dirt of the driveway area—big shoes, by the look of them. The tread had a distinctive pattern. Among the usual lines and rectangles were three star shapes, two on the heel and one big one beneath the ball of the big toe.

But otherwise there was no sight or sound of Bob Bentley—or anyone else.

Of course, he might have made it look that way on purpose. Marsha had insinuated he was lying low, trying to avoid paying back loans he'd defaulted on. *Or he could just be sleeping off a hangover,* Gaia added inwardly as she tripped over a weathered Sam Adams bottle.

She slid her Walther P-38 from its holster and held it out in front of her, taking long but careful strides toward the boat.

"Bob Bentley?" she called out. "Mr. Bentley? This is the FBI. Please come forward."

There was no answer. Only the crackling sounds of the wind through the tree branches and the creaking of the boat in the surf.

Gaia crept down the wooden dock, keeping her gun drawn and her senses primed. There was something ominous about the boat. Something about its faded paint and the way it moaned as it rode the choppy waves. And Mrs. Bentley had been right about the smell. As Gaia stepped closer, a stale, rotting stench grew stronger. She couldn't imagine anyone being able to live in a place that reeked this much. Either Bob had grown used to it—or he was really desperate to get away from the rest of the world.

Soon she reached the end of the dock. "Bob Bentley?" she shouted again as she peered across the empty deck of the boat.

She strained to hear any noises welling up from the cabin below, but there was nothing.

Now what?

Without a warrant or an invitation from the owner, there was no way she could legally board the boat. Considering she was out here without her partner's or supervisors' knowledge, she really should go by the book as much as possible. Yet she knew she had to get on the boat if she wanted any real chance of investigating Bob as a suspect.

Luckily she saw exactly what she needed to see: blood. A trail of brown-red drips that extended from the side of the boat to the door leading down into the hold. Of course, considering this was a fishing boat, the stains could very likely have been made by a particularly drippy sea bass. But blood was blood—only forensics could tell whether it was human or not. She could argue she felt it was better to be safe than sorry.

Still holding her Walther at the ready, Gaia stepped down onto the boat's deck, adjusting her sense of balance as the floor pitched up and down beneath her feet. The wind was picking up and the surf was growing rougher, causing her to lurch unsteadily toward the cabin. Having both hands on her Walther made it even more difficult to maintain her equilibrium. She really, really hoped she didn't have to use the gun. Her aim would be crap in these conditions.

Eventually, after plodding forward in a crooked, drunk-looking fashion, she reached the door to the hold. Keeping her gun in her right hand, she grabbed the knob with her left and slowly twisted it. Almost instantly the door swung inward with a loud squeak, pulling Gaia into a narrow stairwell. She quickly braced herself against the wall, coming to a halt before she could tumble down the rest of the rubber-coated steps. Behind her, the door slammed shut from the motion of the boat.

So much for stealth.

"Mr. Bentley?" she called out. "This is the FBI. If anyone is on board, come out now with your hands where I can see them."

No response. Just the somber creaks and snaps of the boat and the high-pitched howl of the wind outside.

With her back pressed against the left wall, Gaia gradually slid sideways down the remainder of the stairs. Slowly the starboard side of the cabin came into view. There was a pull-down bunk, empty save for a pile of rumpled bedding; a medium-sized chest freezer stained and dented from years of use; and built-in barrister bookshelves crammed with stacks of magazines, various reels and other tackle, and a photo of Cindy Bentley in her high school graduation gown. Next to that, a young blond boy smiled with his baseball glove behind the dusty glass of another picture frame. It looked strikingly like Will. She resisted the urge to touch it.

As soon as her feet hit the rough fiberglass floor, Gaia swung around the wall and pointed her Walther toward the left side of the cabin. The quick movement, combined with the fierce rocking of the boat and overwhelming odor of rotting fish, made Gaia's head reel. Her stomach clenched and a bitter taste bubbled up her throat, and for a couple of seconds her vision blurred. She blinked hard and firmly planted her feet to stop herself from keeling over. Soon her head cleared and the left side of the cabin came into view. Luckily no one was there to take advantage of her weakened state. She took note of the mini-refrigerator, the four cupboards, and the small open closet filled with jeans, flannel shirts, and a pair of thigh-high rubber waders.

No one's here. Unless a big guy like Bob was enough of a contortionist to fit into one of the cabinets or crouch silently inside the narrow toilet stall for several minutes, there was absolutely no place to hide. Besides, the boat just *felt* empty. The chill in the air and the reverberations of her footsteps told her she was definitely the only living thing on board.

"Damn it!" she muttered as she reholstered her gun and plopped down on the third step. If Bob wasn't here, where was he? Should she wait for him? Should she go back to Mrs. Bentley and question her further? Time was running out. If she couldn't come up with any solid evidence to clear Will in the next few hours, Kim would go running to Malloy and Bishop first thing tomorrow.

Gaia closed her eyes, trying to quell the acid that was once again rising up her throat. The mogul-jumping movement of the boat and the sharp, fishy stench that filled the air were really starting to overwhelm her. She couldn't stay on board much longer.

Once her insides felt more settled, she opened her eyes and focused on the floor in front of her. And there, directly in front of her, was another bloodstain. A huge one.

Gaia's heart twanged loudly in her aching head. Instead of a few light splatters, a wide, rust-colored path ran from just below the sink to the nearby dilapidated freezer.

No way that much blood came from fish. Not unless he hooked Moby-Dick.

She carefully rose to her feet and lurched along the swaying floor, following the tracks toward the freezer. Her body was buzzing again—not with fear but with a restless anticipation. Something vital was inside that chest. She just knew it.

As soon as she reached the freezer, she grabbed hold of the metal handle, steadied herself, and threw open the lid. Instead of a welcome puff of cold air, a new, stale stench assaulted her nostrils. The chest obviously didn't work as a freezer anymore, and it was mostly empty except for a few items at the dim depths. Gaia reached in and grasped hold of soft, heavy fabric. Then she lifted her hands to reveal a thick, black wool sweater, reeking of mildew.

Gaia's pulse accelerated. Dark wool! Just like the fibers!

Ignoring the throbbing in her temples, she leaned forward and pulled out two more items: a dark wool hat and something encased in crinkly plastic. Looking closer, she saw it was an economy-sized bag of lollipops—the exact brand used by the killer.

Oh my God, oh my God, ohmyGod! This was it. The proof she'd been searching for. This had to be the Lollipop Killer's lair!

It was all here. Everything she needed to clear Will's name and convince the others that Bob Bentley was the Lollipop Killer. Well . . . *almost* everything she needed.

Where is the knife?

The boat was now bucking even more violently, and strong waves were crashing against the sides with loud splashes. Gaia could feel her stomach capsizing once again.

Just hold on, she told herself as she clamped her throat shut. *Just let me find the weapon.*

Gaia peered back into the freezer, but it was empty. She then staggered into the kitchen area and searched every possible hiding place, every drawer, cabinet, and box. Her frenzied pace coupled with the hurtling motion of the boat was making her dizzy. And her efforts at stemming the vomit bubbling up her throat were fading fast.

If the knife wasn't there and Bob wasn't either, it could mean only one thing: he had it with him. He was planning to kill again, and soon.

She had to warn the others. They needed to put out an APB on Bob Bentley and stop him before he could hurt anyone else.

But first she really, *really* needed to throw up.

that last bit of motivation

Kim paced up and down the narrow corridor, listening to the harsh buzz of the fluorescent lights overhead. Occasionally he paused and stared ominously at one of the doors, the one leading to Will's dorm room. Then, muttering to himself, he would restart his fretful walk, more agitated than before.

He had no idea how long he'd been there, wandering the same four square feet of carpet. Five minutes? Ten? What was he waiting for, anyway? An engraved invitation?

He used to feel just like this before his piano recitals—fully prepared and rehearsed but still nervous as hell. He knew he'd assembled a pretty good amount of evidence against Will, although most of it was circumstantial. He had the handwriting analysis, the references to left-handedness in Gaia's report, remarks made (albeit off the record) by both the transient and the woman at Second Chance who recognized him, and the fact that Will's size and strength matched the killer's. Not to mention Will's occasional angry flare-ups. There was no smoking gun (or in this case, bloody knife), but taken together, it all made a rather convincing portrait of Will as a potential suspect.

At this point, he was pretty certain he had enough proof to take to Bishop and Malloy. Even Gaia seemed to have reluctantly accepted the facts. Here it was coming up on the twenty-four-hour mark and she hadn't even called.

But Kim wasn't quite ready to go to his superiors yet. It would feel too . . . tattletale-ish. Too underhanded. He still had enough of a sense of loyalty toward Will to give him one ultimate chance.

After thinking it over, Kim had decided to talk to Will himself before running to the admin building. It was the right thing to do by a former friend and partner. And besides, evidence aside, he just had to be *sure*. If he confronted Will, he could study his reactions closely—watch for any unconscious movements or body postures. Then Kim would know beyond any doubt whether the guy was guilty or not.

Only . . . it wasn't as easy as he'd thought.

Taking one last deep, fortifying breath, Kim stepped forward and rapped on the door. Then he immediately stepped back and shoved his hands in his jacket pockets, his right hand closing around his concealed Walther. *Just in case.*

He waited several seconds, but there was no answer. Perhaps his knock had been too puny—especially if Will was plugged into his iPod.

Keeping his right hand on his gun, he raised his left and rapped harder. This time he felt it move under the force of his knuckles. The door swung slowly open.

"Will?"

Kim peeked inside. Neither Will nor his roommate was there. The last one to leave must have been in a real hurry. Lights were still on, and the latch hadn't engaged all the way.

His grip relaxed on his gun. So what now?

Well, I tried. I should just go to Malloy and Bishop and show them what I've found, he told himself. Only his feet weren't listening. Kim found himself walking forward, propelled by an overwhelming curiosity . . . and something more. An intense craving for finality, a sense of inevitability. He'd been hoping this visit would give him that last bit of motivation he needed to go against Will—a person he truly cared about in spite of everything.

The room had an odd feeling of interruption about it, as if all life-forms had been vaporized in the middle of their daily routine. The disarray was more spread out than usual. A Coke can sat on the desk beside Will's still-humming laptop, its condensation having completely drenched the papers it sat on.

Kim nudged the mouse, and the computer's starburst screen saver flickered off to reveal Will's e-mail account, still open and active.

Get out of there. You shouldn't be doing this, his conscience scolded loudly.

But Kim ignored it. He was still gripped by that powerful compulsion to face Will. And if he couldn't face the guy himself, perhaps he could still peer into his thoughts.

Glancing around to see if anyone was watching, Kim clicked the back button on the toolbar. The account's Sent folder instantly filled the screen. According to the recorded times, Will had sent a message that morning at a little past eight to Gaia.

"This is so wrong," Kim muttered to himself as he opened up the file, conjuring up the brief, four-sentence e-mail.

Gaia—There's something I have to do. Some unfinished business. It may mean the end of the FBI for me, but I don't know if I care about that anymore. Try to understand. Love—Will

What sort of "unfinished business"? Where had he gone?

As he tried to process this new information, Kim's eyes darted about the room, to the closet, the unmade bed, the wastepaper basket, the tacky South Carolina poster. Suddenly his scanning stopped and reversed, swiveling back to the wastebasket. Something colorful was visible through the wire mesh—something familiar.

He stooped and pulled it out of the can. All at once an icy chill skittered down his spine. It was a greeting card. Blank inside, but on the front was a sweet, scenic photo of a rainbow across a waterfall. The same design as that on each card sent to Ann Bishop, Laurel Halliday, and Terri Barker before they were killed.

Holding tight to the card, Kim raced out of the room and back down the corridor, heading straight for admin. He'd found what he was looking for. He'd had his reckoning. Now there was no doubt in his mind.

Just like Catherine, Will wasn't the person he was pretending to be. Only this time Kim wasn't going to let him slip away.

WARN THEM

After vomiting all over the rocky shoals by the boat dock, Gaia finally felt settled enough to keep moving. She stumbled up the hill toward her car, her head still swirling from seasickness.

When she reached the Cavalier, she took a moment to lean against the car's steel frame and stabilize her ragged breathing. The world was swaying up and down as if she were still on the boat, and she gripped the door handle to prevent herself from falling. Her equilibrium must still be shot. Either that or she was trapped inside a gigantic washing machine.

Eventually she found the strength to grab her cell phone and place a call.

Two rings . . . three rings . . . finally Kim answered. "Gaia, is that you?" His voice had a strange buzzing quality to it, like a radio station slightly off frequency.

"Yeah, it's me." Her words were low and hollow sounding, and her throat felt raw after puking up her morning coffee. "Listen to me, Kim. We need to—"

"You've got to get back here right away," Kim interrupted. "Something's happened. I hate to tell you this on the phone, but we found some more evidence. In Will's room."

Gaia frowned. The heaviness in his voice made her cut short her clamor for an APB. "What did you find?"

His sigh crackled over the line. "A card. The same kind that was sent to the murder victims."

"No!" she snapped, suddenly irritated. This was wrong. Bob Bentley was the killer, not Will.

"I'm afraid it's true. And that's not all. Did you get an e-mail from Will sometime this morning?"

"No." Of course not. She'd been gone since dawn.

"Will went AWOL again, Gaia. He violated probation and left the base without permission."

So? Technically she had, too. She'd signed out as going back to the crime scenes and instead had come searching for Bentley. Will might also have a good explanation.

"I showed Malloy and Bishop everything I had on Will and they freaked," Kim went on in that seventy-mile-an-hour way of his. "They have an APB out on him and everything. Things are crazy here. You've got to get back." He paused and took a breath. "Where are you, anyway?"

"I'm at a beachfront property a few miles southeast of Lake Ridge. It's the Lollipop Killer's hideout, Kim. The murderer isn't Will. It's this guy, Bob Bentley! He had a freezer with knit clothing and lollipops."

"Gaia? What did you say? This connection sucks."

"I said I found a boat!" she yelled into the receiver. "It has an old freezer on it with dark knit clothing and a bag of lollipops inside it!"

There was a slight pause. "Anything else?"

"No," Gaia replied with a scowl. If only she'd found the knife.

He gave another staticky sigh. "I don't know, Gaia. I don't think it's enough to throw them off Will right now. The card—"

"Why is the card such a big deal?" she snapped. "Maybe he just bought it at a local drugstore."

"Not possible," Kim replied. The connection was weakening, and his voice took on a tinny, robotic sound. "This isn't a Hallmark, Gaia. It's made by a small company called Oconee Press. Out of South Carolina."

Gaia slid down the side of the car and sat down on the moist turf. *What?*

"I hope I'm wrong, but I really don't think I am. I'm sorry, Gaia." Gaia could hear some commotion on his end of the line. "I gotta go. Malloy has questions. Get back soon."

Gaia hung up her phone and glanced out at the horizon, blinking hard to push the tears out of her field of vision. Overhead, clumps of dark, leaden-looking clouds rolled through the sky, sapping the landscape of color and warmth. It seemed strangely appropriate—considering she'd just found herself in the middle of a gothic nightmare.

When she found the stash of stuff in the freezer, she'd been so relieved, almost giddy. It meant that she'd finally found the killer and that Will was innocent, just as she had suspected. Only now they'd found that card in his room, and everyone was convinced of his guilt. Even though they were just doing their job, she couldn't help feeling betrayed by Kim and the bureau.

It didn't make sense. How could Will have a card if Bentley was the killer? Why had Will gone AWOL? And where the hell was the knife?

She struggled to her feet. Will was obviously the FBI's lead suspect. He was the one they were throwing all their manpower into tracking down. The only thing she could do was drive back to Quantico and argue her points loud and clear.

Even though her balance still felt slightly off, Gaia climbed into the Cavalier and eased it onto the two-lane highway. She'd barely gone a mile when her cell phone throbbed against her abdomen. *Could they have nabbed Will already?*

She whisked it off her belt and answered it without glancing at the number display. "Yeah?"

"Uh . . . is this Agent Moore?" A male voice crackled over the static. She recognized the gruff, southern tone immediately.

"Yes, this is Agent Moore. Is this Sheriff Parker?"

"Yes, I'm calling to fulfill a promise I made to you earlier."

A promise? "What promise was that?"

"About Terrell Mitchum? Remember you wanted me to let

you know if he made bail?" The sheriff sounded surprised and slightly annoyed.

Right. Now she remembered. At that point she'd been so sure Terrell was the Lollipop Killer.

"We got a call this morning from the Loudon County's sheriff's office. Apparently on the night of the third murder Terrell Mitchum was sleeping off a drunk and disorderly charge in their jail. So I'm calling to let you know he was released about fifteen minutes ago."

Gaia felt a catch in her chest. She'd been wrong about him. She'd been wrong about Catherine. Could this mean she was wrong about Will, too?

"I appreciate you letting me know," she shouted over the increasing static. "Thank you, Sheriff."

"No problem," he drawled before hanging up.

Terrell Mitchum. She'd been so convinced he was the murderer, when all he was guilty of was being a scumbag ex-husband and father. She thought of Kelly and Jasmine. Kelly seemed to believe that Terrell had enough sense not to bother them. Hmmm. Then again, she should probably call and warn them— just to be safe.

Still gripping her phone, Gaia placed another call while keeping her eyes on the road.

"Hello?" came a small, sweet voice over the roaring static.

"Jasmine? Hi, there. It's Gaia."

"Hi! Are you coming to see me?"

Gaia smiled softly. Such an angel. With all she was dealing with, Jasmine's munchkin voice was like therapeutic music.

"No, I can't. I'm sorry. I have to work. Can I talk to your mom really quick?"

"She's in the shower."

"Oh. Well, can you have her call me when she's done? It's really, really important."

"Okay, but she's going on an important rainbow date!" Gaia halted the car abruptly as her chest tightened. "What do you mean?"

"Mama got an invitation to a rainbow date. It was a very pretty card that—" A loud popping noise interrupted her. Jasmine's voice faded beneath a layer of white noise.

"Jasmine!" Gaia shouted. "Tell your mama you have to leave! You have to leave *right now*!" She paused to listen, but there was only a hissing static on the line. "Jasmine? *Jasmine!*"

Gaia hung up and tried to redial, but the phone couldn't find a clear channel.

"Damn it!" she cried, throwing the phone onto the floorboards.

Just then a large water droplet plunked onto the windshield, distorting her view of the road.

A new feeling of foreboding jostled to the forefront. Rain. Didn't Lyle say the killer liked to strike under cover of rain?

Gaia hunched over the steering wheel and pressed the gas pedal to the floor.

THE LOLLIPOP KILLER

Kelly's house had never looked so ominous. In the darkness and rain its sunny yellow paint was undetectable, and the wind made Jasmine's swing twist violently. Even the screen door was creaking like the entrance to an ancient crypt.

As Gaia crept toward the house, keeping her gun out in front of her, she noticed that one light was on upstairs and there was a dim glow emanating from the living room below. Probably the television, she decided. Although she couldn't tell for certain through the thick window drapes.

They better be okay! she thought as the familiar fizzy brew of ultra-concentrated adrenaline coursed through her veins. Her breathing was shallow and rapid, and her jaw was clenched so tightly that her temples were beginning to ache.

She was almost at the back stoop, creeping through the shadow of the maple tree. The sounds of raindrops pecking at the leaves flooded her ears. She crept stealthily up the back porch. The door was already slightly ajar. Gaia pushed it open with the tip of her gun and stepped inside.

The kitchen was completely empty, as was the dining room. But over the steady hum of the rain outside, Gaia could now discern noise drifting down the stairwell: a woman singing, her voice echoing slightly and accompanied by some periodic splashing sounds. Kelly must still be in the shower. Thank God, she was still alive!

As Gaia headed toward the living room, she could make out some additional noises: a high-pitched squawking voice accompanied by several pings, bangs, and boings. Rounding the corner, Gaia could see Jasmine sitting cross-legged in front of the television set, watching an obnoxious cartoon.

Not wanting to confuse or startle the little girl, she decided to survey the room before revealing herself. She stepped forward cautiously, keeping to the shadows. Then she saw them.

Footprints. A heavy, tingly sensation trilled through her. Gaia leaned down and inspected the grimy tread closest to her. There were three distinct stars in the pattern. Two in the heel print and one big one beneath the ball of the big toe. The same tracks she'd seen at the boat dock!

A burst of movement down the hall caught her eye. Gaia trained her Walther on the hulking form.

Stop!" she shouted, her voice thinner, higher than usual.

The figure paused in his path to the stairs, spun around, and glared at her. It was Will, his face half hidden under a woven cap.

"Gaia?" he whispered loudly. "What are you doing here?"

Oh God. Gaia's tingles seemed to morph into knife wounds as doubt rushed over her. Kim had been right. All those clues he'd found, the fact that Will had gone AWOL, the fact that he was here at Kelly's . . . All along Will had been the Lollipop Killer, only she couldn't see it.

She hadn't *wanted* to see it.

The realization hit her like a physical force, and for a moment she couldn't breathe. Her knees buckled slightly, and all that adrenaline—her own heady, specially formulated energy drink—seemed to vaporize from her body, leaving her weak and dizzy.

He pressed a finger to his lips. "No time to explain," he whispered. "I followed a guy here. I'm scared he might be the Lollipop Killer. Come on."

Jasmine jumped to her feet, startled.

"Gaia?" she cried in a shaky voice. Her eyes darted from Gaia to Will's shadowy form and back again. A look of recognition came over Jasmine's face, and she ran toward him, her arms outstretched. "Will!"

Gaia stalked forward, keeping her weapon pointed at Will's chest. "Jasmine, no!" she yelled. "Get away from him!"

Jasmine screamed and shrank back, cowering against the sofa.

"Gaia, what are you doing?" Will whispered loudly.

"Drop your gun, Will," Gaia ordered. "Set it on the floor. *Now.*"

"Gaia?" Will hissed, looking confused and a little irritated. "What the hell . . . ?"

Jasmine was now crying hysterically as she glanced from Gaia to Will and back again. Gaia heard a cadence of footsteps overhead. Kelly must have heard Jasmine's screams and left the shower.

"I said," Gaia repeated, raising her voice, "put down your gun!"

For a couple of seconds Will stood stock-still, refusing to move. "Fine, but you're making a big mistake." He slowly stooped forward and set his gun on the floor.

She stuck out her foot and kicked the gun sideways, sending it spinning across the floor, far out of reach.

"Gaia, *please,*" he begged, sounding incredulous. She had to admit he seemed completely convincing, and for the briefest of seconds she wondered if she might be making a mistake.

"Gaia? Will? What the hell is going on?"

Out of the corner of her right eye Gaia could see Kelly coming down the stairs, her body wrapped in a long white towel. Jasmine leaped to her feet and ran to her mother, pressing her face into the towel and sobbing.

207

"Kelly, take Jasmine and run!" Gaia shouted, still keeping her eyes and gun on Will. "Go get help!"

She saw Will shoot Kelly a flabbergasted expression, as if to imply that Gaia had lost her mind. Kelly hesitated.

"Run!" Gaia went on, her voice shrill with impatience. "You've got to trust me!"

Finally Gaia saw a flurry of motion in the corner of her eye as Kelly picked up Jasmine and ran from the room. Three seconds later Gaia heard the back door slam shut. She exhaled in relief. At least they were safe. She'd come to her senses in time.

"Why?" she asked as she stared into Will's face, the word bubbling up out of her on its own.

She knew she shouldn't engage him. She should force him into a spread-eagle stance and cuff him until help arrived. But at the moment she couldn't move. She was too shot through with pain.

"I honestly don't know what you're talking about," he replied, shaking his head. "Please, Gaia. We have to keep searching the house."

"Just stop it! I *know*," she said, her voice quavering. "I know you're the Lollipop Killer."

"*What?* No! No, listen. The killer is Bob Bentley."

"I know that's the name you used. I saw the boat and the blood. You killed him, didn't you? Then you used his place as your hideout. I saw your tracks. *These* tracks!" She nodded toward the dirty prints on the floor between them.

Will seemed on the verge of losing it. His expression was red and puckered, and his eyes darted all around the room. "*Please!* Keep your voice down!" he hissed. "Yes! I was there. But I was staking him out. I got a card from him with a weird letter inside and tracked down the address." He took a deep, ragged breath. "I saw some suspicious stuff and then followed him here!"

"You . . ." Gaia still couldn't move, and now she couldn't talk. Her mind was a jumble of contradictory information and impulses. Should she trust her instincts and believe him?

"Do you want to see it?" Will asked, his eyes lighting up. "Here. I'll show you the letter." He started to unzip his coat and reach inside.

"Stop!" she shouted, training her gun on him again. "Don't move! Keep your hands where I can—"

All of a sudden Gaia found herself reeling backward, the Walther sailing from her hands into the surrounding shadows. A dark shape had come out of the shadows and crashed into her. She hit the floor, her head banging hard against the hardwood planks. Tiny lights flickered before her eyes and her mouth filled with the bitter, silty taste of blood.

She tried to click into attack mode and roll back onto her feet, but for some reason, she couldn't. She'd been cut off from her power supply after her shock at recognizing the footprints and she still couldn't click into combat mode.

And the shape was coming right at her again.

Gaia heard a rushing noise and instinctively braced for another impact, but it didn't come. She glanced up and shook her head, clearing her vision in time to see two figures struggling. Will and someone else. It was a man; that much she could tell. Bulkier than Will and dressed in dark clothes.

She watched helplessly from her crumpled position as the

bigger guy bent over Will. A second later Will dropped to the floor. The man then turned back toward her, stepping into the faint light of the television. Suddenly she could see his face.

Bob Bentley! He was the Lollipop Killer. Will had been telling the truth!

As he hurtled toward her, Gaia thought of the women he'd murdered and the shattered looks on their children's faces. Raw energy pumped into her limbs and she felt herself fill with a roiling rage.

As soon as Bentley came into range, Gaia caught his momentum and threw him over her head. He crashed upside down into the shelves that held Jasmine's games and then rolled sideways.

Gaia sprang onto her feet and saw him staggering upright, his chest heaving with deep, raging breaths.

The gun! Where's the gun? Gaia's eyes darted from shadow to shadow, searching for the familiar shape of her pistol. But before she could spot it, he was charging at her again.

She sprang out of the way and twisted about, ready to ward off his blows. He quickly righted himself and turned toward her. Something gleamed in his left hand. She hadn't noticed it before with everything moving so fast, but now she could see it clearly. It was a hunting knife, a Yukon Bay double, model sc-42 to be exact, its jagged edge dripping with fresh blood.

Will's blood?

Bentley dove toward her, slashing wildly with his left hand. Gaia ducked and swayed to avoid the blade, her senses keenly pricked to decipher his every move. She calculated diving out of the way, but he was slicing the air too low. She checked the area for something to parry him with, but there was nothing. All she could do was anticipate his actions and avoid his blows.

On and on they jabbed and dodged, crossing the room in a ferocious tango. Gaia was quickly running out of space. With every stroke he was forcing her backward, steering her into a far corner. She fought like a wildcat, desperate to save Will, even if it meant getting herself killed in the process.

Bentley pressed Gaia into the wall. There was nowhere to run, and she felt the sudden chill of her adrenaline reserves sputtering out. He raised his jagged knife. And there was nothing she could do but wait for the blade to fall and pierce her chest.

But at the exact second the knife hit the apex, a loud noise filled the air: the sharp explosion of a gun. Particles of Sheetrock exploded from the wall inches away from her.

Bentley whirled around. *Bang!* A burst from his chest sprayed a hideous wash of blood and flesh on the opposing wall. He wavered for a second and made a strange gurgling noise before falling to the floor with a thunderous crash. Gaia heard the knife skitter across the hardwood floor, and then everything was silent.

Across the hall, Will was lying on his side. His right hand was raised, holding tight to his Walther.

"Will?" Gaia lunged forward and immediately fell to her knees. Her body was giving in to the exhaustion. Consciousness was handing her a pink slip, making her temples throb and clouding her vision with strange fuzzy lines.

The gun clattered from Will's grasp, and he instantly collapsed onto his back.

"Will!" She dragged herself toward him, crawling through the shadowy room toward his inert shape.

As she came within a few inches of him, her hands felt something wet. Glancing down, she saw that she was crawling through a widening channel of dark fluid. It was blood—Will's blood. And lots of it. Blood that had spilled from him as he crawled toward the gun in order to save her.

No! Gaia pulled herself past his shoes, jogging pants, torn jacket, and blood-soaked shirt until she reached his face. His eyes were half closed, and his skin was silvery white. "Hang on! Just hang on!" she cried, bullying her own body as well as his. "Kelly is getting help."

"Gai-aaaah." Will's voice was the barest of whispers.

"I'm here," she said, grasping his hand. It felt limp and cold. "Oh God," she choked, her vision blurring with tears and exhaustion.

"I'm . . . not scared. Just like you . . ." he panted. The corners of his mouth twitched and lifted slightly. "It's what I always wanted. To be your hero . . ."

Will let out a long, rattling breath, and his face fell completely slack. Then something seemed to slam shut behind his eyes, shuttering out all depth and light.

"Will!" she gasped. "I'm sorry," she whispered in a wheezy breath. "I'm so sorry."

Her body was bagging on her. Her energy had completely burned off, and a heavy weight was pressing down on her. Gaia flopped onto her back. Let the sleep come. She didn't want to be here anymore. She didn't want to be anywhere.

She stayed right beside Will, keeping her hand clasped onto his. As her eyelids fluttered, she caught sight of something round and shiny. Lying on the floor beside her was a bright orange lollipop. Gaia blinked and focused, watching its perfect round head sparkle in the half-light. Then everything went dark.

horrible mistakes

A crashing noise woke Gaia with a start. She opened her eyes and tried to focus, but all she could see was white. *What the . . . ? Am I dead?*

Suddenly the white moved to the left. It was a nurse's uniform, with a nurse inside it. She was bending over the table next to Gaia's bed, loudly refilling a green plastic pitcher with ice.

"Ah. I think someone is awake," said a cheerful-sounding voice.

Gaia assumed she was the someone. She lifted her gaze up the white polyester uniform, over the plump hips and fleshy arms to a round, pleasant-looking face. The nurse had gray hair and twinkly blue eyes, and a wide smile had pushed her chubby cheeks into perfect pink balls on either side of her button nose.

"Where am I?" Gaia asked, her voice weak and croaky sounding.

"You're in the campus infirmary," came a reply, a weary male voice.

As the woman stepped back from the bed, Gaia's view widened and she could now see Kim sitting in a chair beside her bed. His face looked puffy from lack of sleep, and his typically perfect hair hung limply around his forehead.

"I'll let you two talk," the nurse announced as she pulled a blue curtain along a track in the ceiling, separating Kim and

Gaia from the rest of the room. Gaia could hear her squeaky footsteps fade into the distance.

"How do you feel?" Kim asked.

"Okay," she replied, struggling onto her elbows. "What happened?"

"You . . . you don't remember?"

Why is he looking at me that way? Kim's expression was so intense. His eyes were jumpy and tentative, yet his expression drooped mournfully, as if the sight of her was almost too heavy for him to manage.

And then suddenly it hit her. Images came at her as if unleashed by invisible floodgate. The rain . . . Kelly's house . . . the fight . . . the gun . . . *Will!*

The memories came at her too fast and strong, and Gaia almost passed out a second time. She sank back into her pillow and closed her eyes. "Bob Bentley attacked Will. Is he . . . ?"

"He was dead when we arrived," Kim replied. His voice was cracked and strained, almost inaudible.

Gaia let the information slowly penetrate. *Will . . . is . . . dead.* Then she waited for the tears, the screams, the compulsion to throw and break objects. But nothing came. She knew the pain was there, lurking in some inaccessible part of her, but otherwise she felt absolutely empty. A complete void. It was as if she, too, were dead.

"I thought Will was the killer," she murmured. "I disarmed him, and then Bentley came out of nowhere." She could see it happening all over again behind her closed lids. "Then Will stepped in and Bentley plunged the knife into him instead of me. Bentley killed him. He was the Lollipop Killer."

Gaia opened her eyes and glared up at the dingy ceiling tiles, still steeped in the memory.

"I know. We all know." Kim let out a long sigh. "I made a huge mistake," he began, his voice low and measured as if he were carefully selecting and dusting off each word before using it. "I really thought Will was . . ." His throat made a faint choking sound and he swallowed hard.

Gaia looked over and saw Kim gazing at the wall with his jaw clenched and his eyes blinking rapidly, obviously fighting off tears. She rummaged through her numbness to see if she had any residual anger toward him, but she didn't. How could she blame Kim when it was her fault Will had been killed?

Kim cleared his throat and sat up straighter. "They found a journal on Bentley confessing to everything. Real sad, sick stuff. Reading through it, you can almost follow him as he slowly loses his mind. He kept up with Will for years after he broke up with his mom, only he never told Will about it. Then at one point, during some recent point of sanity, he wrote Will and asked him for help." Kim paused and hung his head.

Gaia squeezed her eyes shut again. Will had tried to show her that, only she wouldn't let him.

"I'm glad you weren't hurt," Kim went on. "I was so worried when we found you on the floor. You were holding Will's hand. I thought you were both . . . you know."

Gaia glanced at him again. He was still glaring down at the flecked vinyl tiles, as if talking to the Gaia in his memory instead of her. She gingerly pushed herself up to a sitting position and leaned forward, trying to get his attention. "I'm alive, Kim," she said. She could hear the disappointment in her own voice.

She was okay, at least physically. And she didn't want Kim to feel any more guilt than he already was dealing with. He already seemed to be deteriorating before her eyes.

"He loved you," Kim whispered, tears now clearly visible in his eyes. "And you . . . ?" He paused, refusing to finish.

"Yeah." She turned away, unable to meet his gaze any longer. *Yes, Kim. I loved Will.* She had dealt with love and loss before, far too many times. But the pain was never familiar. It always surprised her how much it hurt—like being in the grip of a giant iron claw. She wasn't feeling much yet, but she knew it was coming.

Kim's hand gripped hers firmly. "You want to talk about it?" he asked.

She shook her head. "No."

Keeping his hand on hers, he rose to his feet. "I should probably go tell Malloy you're awake. He was here up until a few minutes ago, pacing and worrying."

"Really?" Gaia almost smiled, trying to envision it.

"Really. And Kelly and Jasmine have been calling every twenty minutes."

"Are they—?"

"They're fine." Kim gave her hand a last squeeze and then let it go. "I've got something important I need to do. You going to be all right?"

"I'm fine. Thanks."

"Okay, then." He stared at her uncertainly. "Bye." Kim pushed the curtain aside and disappeared behind it. A second later his head poked back through the slit. "Gaia?" he said.

"Yeah?"

"I just want to say . . ." He paused and bit his lower lip. "I'm sorry. It might be a while before I can get back to see you. I'll be . . . busy."

Gaia commanded her mouth to bend into a smile. "I understand. It's all right."

He nodded briskly. Then, after locking his sad gaze onto hers for a few more seconds, he turned and walked away.

She waited until his squeaky footsteps faded away. Then she curled up onto her side and stared into the blue of the curtains. Again she was utterly aware of the lack of life inside her. Maybe her insides did die on that cold wet floor in Kelly's house. Maybe from now on instead of just living without fear, she'd have to live with the absence of everything—just an empty human skin. No joy, no pain. And no Will.

Death couldn't have been any worse.

EFFECTIVE IMMEDIATELY

For the second time in as many days, Kim found himself hesitating in front of someone's door.

"Just get it over with," he grumbled. He raised his fist, gave a polite three knocks, and stepped back.

"Enter," came Special Agent Bishop's muffled reply.

Kim pushed open the door and stepped into the room, immediately standing at attention.

"Agent Lau?" Bishop's forehead scrunched in confusion. "What can I do for you?"

"Agent Bishop, I came to . . . to thank you," he began his

217

rehearsed speech, "for this wonderful opportunity at the bureau. In many ways it's been a dream come true for me." He paused and took a breath, suddenly winded and tired, as if he were launching the words out from deep inside him. "However," he continued, "I think it's best for everyone if I resign from your program. Effective immediately."

Kim cleared his throat. His voice had quavered slightly on the word *resign* and then slowly powered down. In case she hadn't heard correctly, he leaned forward and placed his temporary badge and laminated access pass on her desk. Then he resumed his attention stance, resisting the urge to wipe his sweaty palms on his slacks.

Bishop frowned down at the object on her desk and then turned her gaze up to him. "I'm afraid I don't understand, Agent Lau. You said yourself working here was your life's dream. Can you tell me why you are suddenly quitting?"

"It's . . . complicated," he replied, breathy with restrained emotion. "I don't think I could adequately explain it."

Bishop clasped her hands together on her desk and leaned forward. "Humor me," she said, a slight edge to her tone.

Kim sighed and stared down at the carpet, avoiding her gaze. *Just tell her. She needs to know.*

"I don't feel I deserve to be here," he began. "I thought I had a gift—special skills I could bring to the organization. Only . . . I don't seem to have those abilities anymore."

Bishop nodded and leaned back in her chair. "You're referring to your behavior study methods? Your insight into people?"

"Yes, ma'am."

"What makes you think you've lost these talents of yours?"

A huffing noise escaped through his lips. "Isn't it obvious?"

"Again, Agent Lau"—Bishop's voice rose slightly—"please humor me."

Kim had wanted to remain professional; he'd wanted to go out with his dignity intact. But now he found his shoulders slumping as if wilting in defeat, and he absently pulled the fingers of his left hand—a nervous habit that used to drive his piano teacher crazy.

"I've made horrible mistakes," he mumbled hoarsely. "I was completely fooled by Catherine. All that time with her and I never once got suspicious. Never. And now Will . . ." Kim clenched his jaw and took deep breaths, forcing a sob back down inside him. "I accused him of being this horrible thing and he wasn't. And now he's dead. Because of me."

His voice dwindled to a whisper and then diminished altogether. Kim had to close up his throat to hold back another, more powerful wave of emotion.

Bishop's features softened. "Agent Lau, I fail to see how you are responsible for Agent Taylor's death."

Kim opened his mouth and immediately closed it again—unable to speak.

"From what I saw, you did your duty. You gathered evidence and presented it to us. We agreed that it warranted immediate action, but by the time we found Agent Taylor, it was too late."

Kim hung his head. In spite of her businesslike manner, even Bishop's voice sounded reedy.

"And," she went on, "we were also misled by Agent Sanders. I personally thought she was one of our most promising recruits."

He nodded silently. So had he.

"Then I suppose by your reasoning, I should also resign from the bureau?"

Kim's head snapped up. "What? No. No, ma'am. That's ridiculous."

"Is it?" Bishop's eyebrows disappeared beneath her bangs. "I didn't see through Sanders, and I accepted the evidence that pointed toward Taylor. So did Malloy."

"But that's different. You two are . . . I should have . . . I didn't mean . . ." Kim sputtered, his mouth opening and closing like a dying fish's.

Agent Bishop pushed back her chair and rose to her feet. "Agent Lau, nowhere in the FBI rule books does it say that agents have to be perfect. That's something *you* have demanded of yourself. So unless you expect me and Special Agent Malloy to walk out those gates with you, I suggest you grab your things and get back on the job."

Kim could only stand there, blinking into space. Relief and shock took turns squeezing his chest. He didn't have to leave. They were asking him to stay.

But did he want to?

Agent Bishop strode over to him and placed her right hand firmly on his shoulder.

"Pick up your badge and pass, Lau. You'll need them," she said, holding him securely at arm's length and looking him straight in the eye. "And your first assignment for today is to head downstairs and meet with Dr. Lehman. That's an order."

As she gazed at him, supporting him with her surprisingly strong grip, Kim could feel himself slowly reinflate. His insides were still numb, but deep within he sensed a spot of warmth. Perhaps it was hope.

"Yes, ma'am. Right away." With sudden conviction he snatched up his badge and pass and strode to the door, pulling it open. He paused at the threshold and glanced back. "Agent Bishop?"

"Yes, Lau?" she said, settling back at her desk.

"I just wanted to say . . . thanks."

"You're welcome, Agent." She smiled warmly at him for the briefest of seconds before her face reverted back to its usual blank, no-nonsense expression. "Now get back to work. We need you."

THE FBI'S WALKING DEAD

"Have you been sleeping well?"

"Pretty much."

"Have you been eating?"

Gaia blinked mawkishly at Dr. Lehman. "Yes, Mom."

He didn't seem at all amused. Dr. Lehman seemed to be all business today. The whole session so far had a sense of urgency about it. As if she were in some sort of critical state and he needed to do the psychological equivalent of CPR on her mind. It had been a month since she lost Will. And she had thought things would have gotten easier by now. But most of the time Gaia felt like a shell-shocked version of her former self.

"Any dreams at night?" he went on.

Gaia shrugged. "None that I remember."

"What about your waking thoughts? Do you think about Will much?"

"Yes," she replied, suddenly irritable. It was such a dumb question. How could she *not* think about him? Even when she didn't purposefully remember, all sorts of things reminded her of him. And sometimes it just came out of nowhere. There'd be no particular trigger, yet entire flashbacks would start rolling inside her head like her own little mental film fest.

Dr. Lehman paused to write something on a notepad, and Gaia found herself panting. *It's happening again,* she thought as images of Will began flooding her mind. Will whispering in her ear as they held each other in bed. Will staring at her in shock and disappointment as she trained her Walther on him. Happy Will. Sad Will. Alive Will. Dead Will.

"Tell me," he went on. "When you think about Will, how do you feel?"

Gaia scowled and stared off in the direction of the bookcase. Another stupid question. "I feel bad."

"Can you be more specific? What exactly are your feelings?"

What *weren't* her feelings? Lately it seemed like she was experiencing every awful emotion in the lexicon, and all of them simultaneously.

At least she was feeling something. For a while there had been nothing but an intense hollowed-out sensation, and she'd trudged about the corridors as if stupefied—the FBI's walking dead. But now it seemed to be wearing off, like a fading cloud cover, allowing all those emotions to penetrate. And with them came a constant scorching pain.

"I'm sad, I guess," she said, trying to choose the main sentiment in the whole heady mix.

He leaned forward in his chair. "Sad about what? For whom?"

"I'm sad for everyone in this crappy mess. But mostly for Will. He didn't deserve this." Her voice broke suddenly, surprising her. She hadn't cried yet. She'd been too numb, too overwhelmed. Only now Dr. Lehman and his leading questions were making her dive right into her emotional whirlpool and confront things head-on.

Normally she owned these situations. If she didn't want to analyze something, she didn't have to. And there hadn't been a single therapist who could make her. But for some reason, her shields just wouldn't go up.

A few rogue tears formed in the corners of her eyes, and she angrily brushed them away with her hands. Dr. Lehman handed her a box of Kleenex while keeping his understanding gaze on her. She knew he was waiting for her to continue. Waiting for her to explode.

"But it's more than that. I'm also sad that instead of just mourning Will, I'm mourning someone else I've lost. An ex-boyfriend." She closed her eyes and breathed deeply. She could see their faces in her mind, like a haunted gallery. Jake. And Will. Jake-Will. They almost seemed to be merging. "I guess that sounds weird, huh?" she asked as she opened her eyes. "It almost seems like Will is getting cheated out of some of my grief."

"That doesn't sound weird," Dr. Lehman said. His rich melodic voice was immensely calming, yet for some reason, her tears began to spill out faster. "Tragedies often dredge up past losses. No one is judging you, Gaia. You have the right to feel what you feel."

A flash of annoyance masked her sadness, and for a moment the tears stopped. "But those losses are all my fault. No one would have gotten hurt if it weren't for me."

Dr. Lehman's eyebrows flew to the middle of his forehead, as if he was surprised or slightly bemused. "So, what's the alternative?" he asked. "To shut down and never let anyone get close to you? Isn't it better to just do our best and accept that we can't stop everything awful from ever happening to people we know?"

Gaia stared down at the mangled Kleenex in her hands. She'd been told this before. People always made it sound so simple: Acknowledge that you can't save the world! You're only human! You're one against the forces of nature! Blabbity blah!

When horribly unfair things happened, people shrugged them off too easily. But she refused to play pretend. Why put on a happy face? That sort of denial just wasn't her, and she never could see the value in it.

Dr. Lehman was frowning, his lower lip again jutting forward as he scrutinized her. "You need to put this behind you Gaia," he said. "You need to make peace with what happened and move on. Otherwise it will affect you deeply. Not only as an agent, but as a person."

"Are you saying if I don't, you won't declare me fit for field duty?"

"I'm saying you won't *be* fit for field duty." He sat forward, his features sagging with warm concern. "You can't carry this around with you. I know you think you have to—that you have to burden yourself as part of some great penance. But it doesn't work that way. If you don't let this go, it will slowly poison you until you can't function. Then you won't be able to help anyone ever again.

Will is gone, Gaia. You have to stop trying to save him—*and* all the people in your past."

A stinging sensation swept over Gaia. It was as if each of his words had taken solid form and then hurled themselves against her, pummeling her from head to toe. Memories crashed through her mind. Will and Jake. Jake and Will. Jake-Will. Two boys she loved, dying . . . And then all at once a searing pain swarmed into the center of her chest—as if she, too, had been shot or stabbed along with them.

The hurt was conquering her, sending shudders through her body and clamping tightly around her throat. At the same time, an intense pressure was building behind her ribs, threatening to erupt into loud sobbing. Gaia struggled to contain it. A few renegade tears were one thing, but she never ever allowed herself to blubber in front of other people. *Never.*

Then a new memory washed over her. One where she'd cried without reserve, in a dark New York City alley. In the arms of someone she'd trusted and loved but had ultimately left behind.

Ed.

"It's okay, Gaia," Dr. Lehman said. "Let it come out."

That was all it took. Gaia flashed the doctor one final death glare, which turned into a shuddery, helpless stare, and the next thing she knew she was doubled over, crying uncontrollably.

She wept for Will and everything he would never get to be. Then she wept for Jake. Beautiful Jake who had loved her more than she deserved. Then she wept for Ed, who'd begged her not to say goodbye. They were all gone from her life , without dignity or closure.

It was the definition of unfair.

"It's all right," Dr. Lehman said. "Let it out and let it go."

After an unknowable amount of time, Gaia's sobs gradually subsided and most of the agonizing pressure had lifted. Now she just felt raw and tender and really, really puny.

"How do you feel?"

She frowned at Dr. Lehman's blurry outline. "Like crap."

"It's tough, I know. It will take some time. But you're doing a good job of releasing. It's the first step of letting it all go."

"But I don't want to let it all go!" she snapped. "I don't want to forget about them!"

"Of course you don't want to forget them," he continued. "But you do their memory a disservice by only focusing on their deaths. Don't punish yourself, Gaia. You let these people into your life to learn something from them."

Gaia dabbed at her runny nose. He was right, sort of. At least that part made sense.

"How about we spend some time talking about Will? Just the good stuff," Dr. Lehman said. "Feel up to it?"

Gaia closed her eyes and exhaled slowly. A picture of Will appeared in her mind. Only it wasn't the haunting sight of his bloody, broken body. Instead it was Will vibrantly alive, laughing and joking and grinning that cocky grin of his. "Yes. Okay," she said, opening her eyes. "I think I'd like that."

Gaia

Will. Dear Will. Forgive me. I still love you and miss you and will hurt forever over losing you.

For the longest time I envisioned my heart as some sort of bauble—a fragile piece of porcelain that shattered when Jake died and then was reassembled with liberal amounts of Elmer's glue. I assumed if I ever took it back out and used it, I'd run the risk of busting it all over again. Only now I realize that analogy isn't quite right. My heart isn't some brittle gift-shop trinket. It's more like . . . a starfish. It suffered a horrible disfiguring blow when Jake was killed, but then it regenerated itself—made itself anew. It was never exactly the same, but it worked.

I know because I used it on you. I fell for you and then I lost you. But somehow it wasn't the end of me. I'm still here. I'm mad and screwy and intensely sad, but I've still got life in me.

For years I've been licking these wounds, and now I realize I've been using all the loss in my life as a monumental excuse for everything. I resisted getting too close to people, like Ed. I avoided revealing too much about my past, kept that mutilated of heart of mine in a dark, dusty corner. I don't want to use your death as an excuse. You or Jake or Mom or anyone else who was taken from me.

For a girl with no fear I certainly was running from a hell of a lot.

Now I'm learning to share. Not just my strengths, and not just innocuous things like birthdates and shoe sizes, but everything. Grief and guilt and maybe a secret or two. It started with me admitting my fearlessness to you. And I can't let it stop there.

I'll never forget you, Will. I'm moving forward because you saved me, even though I have no idea where I'll end up. I do know one thing, though. I'm no longer going to keep my heart under lock and key. As shabby and dilapidated as it is, I'm going to share it, too.

Because it's not just about me anymore either.

Gaia's hand lifted the receiver for the millionth time that morning. Her palms were so sweaty, the phone nearly slipped out from her clammy grip. She listened to the hum of the dial tone as she crossed her room and pressed her forehead against the glass window.

She peered down at one of Quantico's winding pathways. It looked like a university quad from a glossy brochure, with people walking briskly, chatting, smiling, and enjoying a typical sunny morning. Gaia couldn't help feeling like she was a completely different species. Would she ever feel totally comfortable again moving among them, or would she always feel like a fake?

It had been another month since her mini-breakdown in Dr. Lehman's office. Little by little she was getting okay with human contact again. She'd gone to the campus gym a few times with Kim for a good old-fashioned sweat fest. She'd exchanged several letters with her brother, and three days ago she'd had a two-hour phone conversation with her father. Yesterday she'd finally taken Kelly up on her offer to escape the base for an afternoon of girly delights.

"That's what today is all about," Kelly had urged. "Forgetting all our cares and just having fun!"

"Yeah," Gaia half cheered, trying unsuccessfully to match Kelly's enthusiasm.

What was so bad about spending a day with Kelly, shopping and getting something called a "beauty treatment"? Although

Gaia had never been much of a mall rat and her beauty regimen usually only consisted of a good hairbrushing, Kelly should have been a great distraction.

But that was just it. She *knew* that Kelly was wonderful and she should enjoy spending time with her, but she just couldn't *feel* it. Even though her regular sessions with Dr. Lehman were helping relieve the pain and guilt, she still couldn't feel anything resembling real happiness or even contentment. There was definitely something missing, and Gaia wondered if she'd ever get that something back.

When the operator's tinny voice instructed her to please try her call again, Gaia ignored the sudden catch in her chest, depressed the receiver, and stared back out her window.

Her mind lapsed into a detached, fugue-like state. It had been her best strategy for coping the last several weeks. Instead of thinking about death and murder and heartbreak and isolation, she focused on more mechanical things. Like eating, flossing, or organizing her sock drawer. Last night, after Kelly had dropped her off with newly polished fingernails, skin glowing from a Black Sea mud mask, and a new pair of designer jeans, she'd gone through some old boxes lurking deep in her closet out of stir-crazy boredom. And that's when she'd found it—her Village School yearbook.

It was a Pandora's box of uncomfortable memories, with gold type on the navy blue hardcover. Gaia had promised herself that she'd never return to New York, but the temptation to revisit her past from the safety of her bedroom was impossible to resist.

She flipped through the smiling portraits of Heather, Sam, Kai, and Ed. Her mind wandered back to the senior prom she'd missed.

The fancy dresses, slow dances, the hugs and promises to keep in touch. It was a rite of teen passage that she'd never experienced.

Instead Gaia's prom night had consisted of a tearful back-alley goodbye with Ed, once he realized she wasn't going to shoot him in the head for his wallet. He'd begged her to stay and not to bail like she had the night they shared everything. Consumed with remorse, she'd pledged that if she could live that moment over again, she would have stayed with him. And they'd shared one last, wonderful kiss.

But that hadn't stopped her from running though Times Square to catch a bus in the dirty bowels of Port Authority. Gaia had wanted to make New York a piece of her history, and her leaving was a decision she never thought she'd regret. But the more Gaia reminisced about her goodbye with Ed, the more she wondered if her desire to disappear into thin air was just one more domino in the chain reaction of how her life had gone to hell.

But the truth was that Gaia really hadn't disappeared. She was right here, alive thanks to Will, with a life to live to its fullest in his honor.

Was it really too late for her?

Gaia looked down at the phone. Something instantly stirred within her—a small but growing flame that warmed her insides and made her mouth stretch into a small smile.

"Hello. It's Gaia," she practiced. "This is Gaia calling. Um, this is Gaia Moore. I hope I'm not catching you at a bad time." Just the sound of her own voice, though somewhat shaky, convinced Gaia she could get through to tomorrow. It made her truly fearless . . . she was ready to stop running.

Her fingers punched numbers recalled from deep in the recesses of her memory. After a few rings a familiar voice on the other end of the phone said hello. The last thing she'd heard him say was goodbye.

She took a deep breath. It had been such a long time.

"Hi, Ed. It's Gaia."

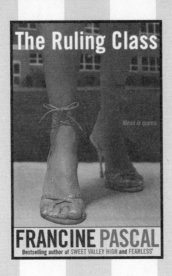